# NECKLACE AND CALABASH

Due to its proximity to the Water Palace, the summer residence of the Emperor's favourite daughter, Rivertown lies within a Special Area administered by the military. To Judge Dee, returning to his district of Poo-yang, the peaceful riverside town promises a few days' fishing and relaxation.

But it is not to be. A chance meeting with a Taoist recluse, a gruesome body fished out of the river, strange guests at the Kingfisher Inn, a princess in distress—before long the judge is facing one of the most intricate and baffling mysteries of his career.

BOOKS BY ROBERT VAN GULIK

*The Emperor's Pearl*
*The Haunted Monastery*
*The Lacquer Screen*
*The Red Pavilion*
*The Willow Pattern*
*The Monkey and the Tiger*
*The Phantom of the Temple*
*Murder in Canton*

*Necklace and Calabash*

# NECKLACE AND CALABASH

*A Chinese Detective Story*

by

ROBERT VAN GULIK

*With eight illustrations*
*drawn by the author in Chinese style*

Charles Scribner's Sons     New York

Printed in the United States of America
SBN 684-10620-5
Library of Congress Catalog Card Number 78-140392

# ILLUSTRATIONS

# DRAMATIS PERSONAE

Note that in Chinese the surname—here printed in capitals—precedes the personal name.

| | |
|---|---|
| Judge DEE | Magistrate of the district of Pooyang, who is staying two days in Rivertown while returning to his post |
| The Third Princess | the Emperor's favourite daughter, who resides in the Water Palace, east of Rivertown |
| Hydrangea | Chief Lady-in-waiting |
| LEI Mang | Chief Eunuch of the Water Palace |
| WEN Tung | Superintendent of the Water Palace |
| Colonel KANG | Commander of the Imperial Guard |
| Captain SIEW | his assistant |
| WEI Cheng | host of the Kingfisher Inn |
| TAI Min | cashier of that inn |
| Fern | Wei Cheng's niece |
| LANG Liu | a wealthy silk merchant |
| Master Gourd | a Taoist monk |

# I

When Judge Dee had ridden for another hour through the hushed, dripping forest he halted his horse and cast a worried look at the dense foliage overhead. He could see only a small patch of the leaden sky. The drizzle might change into a summer shower any time; his black cap and black-bordered brown travelling-robe were wet already, and moisture glistened on his long beard and side-whiskers. When he had left the village at noon he had been told that if he took a right turn at each fork in the road through the forest he would arrive in Rivertown in ample time for the evening rice. He must have taken a wrong turn somewhere, for he estimated he had been riding for about four hours now, seeing nothing but the tall trees and the thick undergrowth, and meeting no one. The birds had stopped singing in the black branches, and the odour of wet, rotting leaves seemed to cling to his very clothes. Wiping his beard and whiskers with the tip of his neck-cloth, he reflected dismally that it would be awkward if he were really lost, for dusk was falling and the forest spread for miles on end along the south bank of the river. The chances were that he would have to spend the night out in the open. With a sigh he uncorked the large brown calabash hanging by a red-tasselled cord from his saddle, and took a draught. The water was luke-warm and tasted stale.

He bent his head and wiped his eyes. The sweat from his moist brow was hurting them. When he looked up he suddenly stiffened, and stared, incredulous, at the hulking shape riding towards him on a horse that trod noiselessly on the soft moss. His perfect double: a man with a long beard and whiskers, wearing a square black cap and a black-bordered brown travelling-robe. Hanging from his saddle by a red-tasselled cord was a large brown calabash.

Again he rubbed his eyes. When he looked a second time he

sighed with relief. The uncertain light and his sore eyes had deceived him. The other's beard and whiskers were streaked with grey, and he rode an old, long-eared donkey. Then the judge was on the alert again. Two short pikes were lying across the donkey's rump. His hand moved to the hilt of the sword hanging on his back.

The man pulled up in front of Judge Dee's horse and glared at him, a brooding glint in his large eyes. His broad face was wrinkled, and though he carried himself well his bony shoulders stood out under the worn, patched robe. What the judge had taken to be pikes now proved to be a pair of crutches with crooked ends. He let go of his sword and asked politely:

'Is this the road to Rivertown, venerable sir?'

The other did not reply at once. His eyes had strayed to the calabash hanging from Judge Dee's saddle. Then he smiled. Fixing the judge with his strange, lacklustre eyes, he said in a surprisingly sonorous voice:

'Yes, eventually it'll take you to Rivertown, Doctor. By a detour.'

The old man was taking him for a physician, evidently because the judge was travelling all alone, and because of the gourd, which is commonly used by doctors to carry their potions. Before he could set the other right, he had resumed:

'I just left town by the short cut, a little further on. I'll gladly show you the way, for it'll take only a quarter of an hour.' Turning his donkey round, he muttered, 'We'd better see about the man they found in the river. He might need your attention, Doctor.'

Judge Dee was going to say that he was the Magistrate of Poo-yang, the district in the northern part of the province, but he reflected that he would then have to explain at length to his casual acquaintance why he was travelling in such simple attire, and without official retinue. So instead he just asked:

'What is your honourable profession, sir?'

'I have none. I am just a vagrant monk. Of the Taoist creed.'

'I see. I had taken you for a colleague. What have you got in that calabash?'

'Emptiness, sir. Just emptiness. More valuable than any potion you might carry in yours, Doctor! No offence meant, of course. Emptiness is more important than fullness. You may choose the finest clay for making a beautiful jar, but without its emptiness that jar would be of no use. And however ornate you make a door or window, without their emptiness they could not be used.' He drove his donkey on with a click of his tongue, then added, as an afterthought, 'They call me Master Gourd.'

The fact that the other was a Taoist monk, and therefore indifferent to all normal civilities, absolved the judge completely from telling him his real name and profession. He asked:

'What were you saying about a person found in the river?'

'When I was leaving town I heard that a man had been brought ashore by two fishermen. This is the short cut. I'll ride in front.'

The narrow forest path led to a cultivated field where, hunched in his straw raincoat, a farmer was digging up weeds. A muddy track took them to the road that ran along the riverfront. The drizzle had stopped, and now a thin mist was hovering over the wide expanse of brown water. Not a breeze stirred in the hot, damp air that weighed down from the low sky. Neat-looking houses lined the road, and the passers-by were well dressed. There wasn't a single beggar about.

'Looks like a prosperous town,' the judge remarked.

'It's a small town, but it profits from the traffic on the river, the good fishing, and the custom from the Water Palace. That's one of the imperial detached palaces, to the east of the town, over on the other side of the pine forest. This western part of the town is the poorer section. The well-to-do live in the east quarter, beyond the fish-market over there. I'll show you the two best inns, the Kingfisher and the Nine Clouds. Unless you are planning to stay with a relative or friend. . . .'

'No, I am a stranger here, just passing through. I see you carry a pair of crutches. What's wrong with your legs?'

'One is lame, and the other isn't too good either. Nothing you could do anything about, Doctor! Well well, the authorities are on the spot. Alert as ever! That means that the man they fished

3

out of the river won't need your assistance, Doctor! But let's have a look anyway.'

On the broad quay in front of the fish-market, by the ferry-house, a small crowd had gathered. Over their heads the judge saw the erect figure of a horseman. The gilt, red-plumed helmet and red neckcloth proclaimed him a captain of the Imperial Guard.

Master Gourd grasped his crutches, climbed down from his donkey and hobbled towards the crowd. The donkey let one ear hang down, and began to search for scraps of garbage among the cobble-stones. Judge Dee alighted from his horse and followed the old monk. The onlookers made way for him; they seemed to know him well.

'It's Tai Min, the cashier of the Kingfisher, Master Gourd,' a tall fellow said in a low voice. 'Dead as a doornail, he is.'

Two guardsmen in their long coats of mail held the crowd at bay. Judge Dee looked over Master Gourd's shoulder at the man sprawled on the ground right in front of the captain's horse. He winced involuntarily. He had often been witness to violent death, but this corpse presented a particularly sickening sight. It was a young man, clad only in a long-sleeved jacket that stuck to his stretched-out arms. Long strands of wet hair clung to his bloated, horribly distorted face. His bare legs and feet had been badly burnt; his hands were mangled. His belly had been slit and the pale intestines were hanging out. A lieutenant was kneeling by the side of the corpse, his back very broad under the curving, gilt shoulder-pieces.

'There's a flat package in his left sleeve!' a hoarse voice spoke up. 'Must be my silver!'

'Shut up!' the lieutenant barked at the gaunt man with the beaked nose and ragged beard who was standing in the front row.

'That's Wei Cheng, the owner of the Kingfisher,' Master Gourd whispered to the judge. 'Always thinks of money first!'

Judge Dee gave the lanky innkeeper a cursory look. Then his eyes fell on the girl standing by his side. He put her at about seventeen, small and slender in a long blue robe with a red sash, her glossy black hair done up in two simple coils. She had turned

4

her head away from the dead man, her handsome face chalk-white.

The lieutenant righted himself. He said respectfully to the captain:

'The condition of the body does indeed point to its having been in the water for a day, sir. What are your orders?'

The captain didn't seem to have heard him. The judge could not see his face well, for he had pulled the red neckcloth up over his mouth. His heavy-lidded eyes were fixed on the riding-whip in his tightly closed, mailed fist. He sat there, slim in his gilt cuirass, immobile as a bronze statue.

'What are your orders, sir?' the lieutenant asked again.

'Have the body taken to headquarters,' the captain said in a muffled voice. 'With the fishermen who found it. And the inn-keeper who employed the victim.'

The captain swung his horse round, so abruptly that the on-lookers behind him had to jump aside to avoid being trampled down. He rode towards the broad street leading away from the quay, the hoofs of his horse clattering on the wet cobble-stones.

'Stand back, all of you!' the lieutenant barked.

'A despicable murder!' Judge Dee remarked to Master Gourd as they walked back to their mounts. 'The man was a civilian, though. Why do the military deal with the case instead of the magistrate of this district?'

'There's no magistrate in Rivertown, Doctor. Because of the Water Palace, you see. The town and its surroundings are what is called a Special Area, administered by the Imperial Guard.' He climbed on his donkey and laid the crutches across its rump. 'Well, I'll say good-bye here. You just ride down the street the captain took; it's the town's main thoroughfare. You'll find the two hostels a little beyond the Guard's headquarters. The King-fisher and the Nine Clouds face each other across the street there. Both are comfortable—take your choice!' He clicked his tongue and rode off before the judge could even thank him.

Judge Dee walked his horse over to the blacksmith at the corner of the fish-market. The animal needed a good rest. He gave the blacksmith a handful of coppers and told him to give the horse a

5

rub down and feed it. He would come to fetch it the next morning.

Entering the main street, he suddenly realized that his legs were stiff from the long ride, and his mouth was parched. He went into the first tea-house he saw and ordered a large pot of tea. Half a dozen citizens were gathered round the larger table in front of the window. They were talking animatedly while cracking dried melon-seeds. Sipping his tea, Judge Dee reminded himself that, since he was here in a Special Area subject to strict security regulations, he was required to register at the Guard's headquarters as soon as he had arrived. He would do that on his way to the hostels, for according to the old monk they were located a little way beyond the headquarters. Since the cashier of the Kingfisher had been tortured and killed in such an abominable manner, everybody there would, of course, be upset. He had better take a room in the other hostel, the Nine Clouds. The name Kingfisher sounded attractive, though; he had actually planned to do some fishing during his two days in Rivertown. In Poo-yang he could never find time for it. Stretching his legs, he reflected that the military would probably catch the murderers of the cashier soon enough. The military police were very efficient as a rule, although their methods were considered crude compared to those of the civilian authorities.

More guests came drifting inside. Judge Dee caught some fragments of their conversation.

'Wei is talking nonsense,' an elderly shopkeeper said. 'Tai Min was no thief. I used to know his father, the old grocer.'

'Highwaymen would never have attacked him if he hadn't been carrying a lot of silver,' a young man remarked. 'And he sneaked out of town in the middle of the night. The blacksmith told me so himself. Tai rented a horse from him. Had to go and see a sick relative, Tai said.'

They settled down in the far corner.

The judge poured himself another cup of tea. He wondered about the antecedents of Master Gourd. The old monk seemed a cultured gentleman. But he knew that since Taoist monks are not bound by any monastic rules, many elderly scholars who find themselves alone and disenchanted with the world adopt their

6

vagrant life. The tea-house was getting crowded now; there was a confused babble of voices. A waiter began to light the oil-lamps, and their smoke mingled with the smell of wet clothes. The judge paid and left.

A drizzling rain was coming down. He bought a sheet of oiled cloth at the street-stall opposite and, draping that over his head and shoulders, he quickly walked down the busy street.

Two blocks farther on, the main street broadened out into an open square. In its centre stood a large, fortress-like building of three storeys. A red-and-blue banner hung down limply from the pointed, blue-tiled roof. On the awning over the red-lacquered gate was written in large black letters: 'Imperial Guard. Second Regiment of the Left Wing'. Two guardsmen stood at the top of the greystone steps, talking with the burly lieutenant whom Judge Dee had seen on the quay. Just as the judge was going to ascend the lieutenant came down and told him in a clipped voice:

'The captain wants to see you, sir. Please follow me.'

Before the astonished judge could say a word, the lieutenant had disappeared round the corner of the building. Quickly unlocking the narrow door of the watch-tower, he pointed up a flight of steep, narrow stairs. While the judge was going up, he heard the lieutenant put the iron bar across the door below.

## II

In the half-dark corridor on the second storey the lieutenant knocked on a plain wooden door. He ushered the judge into a spacious, bare room, lit by a tall candle on the simple writing-desk at the back. The squat young captain who was sitting behind it jumped up and came to meet the judge.

'Welcome to Rivertown, Magistrate Dee!' he said with a broad smile. 'I am Captain Siew. Please be seated!'

Judge Dee gave him a sharp look. He had a full, intelligent face, adorned by a small black moustache and a stiff, jet-black chinbeard. He couldn't place him at all. Pointing at the armchair by the desk, the captain resumed:

'You were kept far too busy to notice me, sir, two years ago! It was in Han-yuan, when you were winding up the lake murders there. I was on the staff of the Imperial Inquisitor, you know.' And to the lieutenant, 'That's all, Liu! I'll look after the tea myself.'

Judge Dee smiled faintly, thinking of that hectic day in Han-yuan*. He laid his sword on the wall-table and took the chair the captain had offered him. 'You recognized me on the quay, I presume?'

'Yes, sir. You were standing beside our good Master Gourd. Didn't like to address you then and there, because you seemed to be travelling incognito. Knew you'd be coming to my office to register anyway, sir, and told my assistant to be on the look-out for you. You are on a special mission, I presume, sir? Travelling all alone . . .' He let the sentence trail off, poured a cup of tea, and sat down behind his desk.

'Oh no. I was summoned to the prefecture ten days ago, to assist the prefect in dealing with a smuggling case affecting my

* See the novel The Chinese Lake Murders.

district. He kept myself and my two lieutenants Ma Joong and Chiao Tai quite busy, and gave me permission to travel back to Poo-yang in a leisurely manner. We had planned to stay a couple of days here in Rivertown. But when we arrived in the village of Kuan-ti-miao this morning, the headman asked us to do something about the wild boars that are spoiling their crops. Ma Joong and Chiao Tai are excellent hunters, so I told them to stay behind and have a go at the wild boars, while I rode on. They are due to join me here the day after tomorrow. I plan to have a rest here, do a bit of fishing or so. Strictly incognito, of course.'

'Excellent idea, sir! How did you get hold of that gourd, by the way?'

'A souvenir the village headman pressed on me. They raise particularly large gourds there in Kuan-ti-miao. My carrying it made Master Gourd mistake me for a travelling physician!'

The captain gave his guest a thoughtful look. 'Yes,' he said slowly, 'you might easily be mistaken for a doctor, in your present garb.' After a slight pause he resumed, 'Master Gourd must have been disappointed when he learned you weren't a physician. He knows a lot about medicinal herbs, and likes to talk about them.'

'As a matter of fact,' Judge Dee said, a little self-consciously, 'I didn't undeceive him. It saved me a long explanation, you see. Who is he, really?'

'A kind of philosopher; has been about here for the last four or five years. Lives like a hermit, in a hut somewhere in the forest. Have another cup, sir!' The captain scratched his nose. Darting a quick glance at the judge, he went on, 'Well, if you really want to have a quiet time here in our town, sir, I advise you to stick to your physician's role. This being a Special Area, there are all kinds of government agents about, and your incognito might be eh . . . misinterpreted, so to speak. I once was a special service man myself, and I know their mentality!'

The judge pulled at his moustache. As a visiting magistrate he would have to make official calls, all dressed up in his ceremonial robe and winged cap—and they were still in Kuan-ti-miao with his heavy luggage. He could borrow a set, of course, and rent an official palankeen, but this was exactly the sort of thing he wanted

9

to get away from for a few days. . . . Captain Siew noticed his hesitation, and resumed quickly:

'I'll fix everything for you, sir! You are fully entitled to a few days of rest. Heard all about that case of the Buddhist temple you solved in Poo-yang. Fine piece of detecting, sir!* Let me see, now. Yes, I know a retired doctor in the capital, Liang Mou his name is. Tall fellow, long beard. Specialist in lungs and liver.' He pulled a sheet of paper towards him, moistened his writing-brush and jotted down a few lines. 'You have studied a bit of medicine, of course, sir? Fine! May I have your identity document?'

Judge Dee pulled the paper from his riding-boot and put it on the desk. 'I don't think . . .' he began. But the captain was absorbed in his study of the document. Looking up, he exclaimed:

'Couldn't be better, sir! Birth-date fits, more or less!' He rapped his knuckles on the desk and shouted, 'Liu!'

The lieutenant came in at once, apparently he had been waiting just outside the door. The captain gave him his note together with Judge Dee's identity document. 'Make out a new one, in this name, Liu. Not too new, though, eh!'

The lieutenant saluted and went out. Captain Siew put his elbows on the desk.

'Fact is, I am faced with a little problem, sir,' he said earnestly. 'Your being here incognito would help me to solve it. Wouldn't take much of your time, and you'd be doing me a tremendous favour, sir! You rank much higher than me, of course, but our work being similar, so to speak. . . . Would help me no end, sir! I always say that in order to get a fresh look at things. . . .'

'You'd better explain what your problem is,' Judge Dee interrupted dryly.

The captain got up and went to the large map on the wall. From where he sat the judge could see that it showed the area south of the river, with a detailed plan of the town. To the east there was a blank square, marked in large letters 'Water Palace'. With a sweep of his arm Captain Siew said:

* See the novel *The Chinese Bell Murders*.

10

'The entire Special Area is under the direct administration of the Palace. You know of course, sir, that for four years now the Water Palace has been the summer residence of the Third Princess.'

'No, I didn't.' But Judge Dee knew about the Third Princess. She was the Emperor's favourite daughter, said to be exceedingly beautiful. The Emperor granted her every wish, but apparently she was not the spoilt palace-doll one might expect, but a very intelligent, level-headed young woman who took a deep interest in the arts and sciences. Various prominent young courtiers had been mentioned as future imperial sons-in-law, but the Emperor had always postponed a decision. The Princess must now be about twenty-five, the judge thought. Captain Siew continued:

'The highest authorities here are three officials, two civil and one military. The Chief Eunuch is responsible for the Third Princess, her court-ladies and all their womenfolk. Then we have the Palace Superintendent who is responsible for the rest of the personnel, a thousand persons in all. My chief, Colonel Kang, is the Commander of the Guard. He is in charge of the security of the palace, and the rest of the Special Area. He has his offices in the palace and is fully occupied with his work there. So he has assigned two hundred guardsmen to me, and put me in charge of the administration of the town and the countryside. It's a quiet, orderly little town, for in order to prevent epidemics from spreading to the palace no brothels are allowed here, no streetwalkers, no theatres, and no beggars. Crimes are rare, because any offence committed here could be construed as lese-majesty, and be punished with the "lingering death". And not even the most hardened criminal wants to risk being sliced to pieces slowly! Ordinary executioners take only two or three hours over the process, but those in the palace can keep their man alive for a couple of days, I am told.' The captain rubbed his nose reflectively, then added, 'They are the best that can be had, of course. Anyway, the result is that all robbers, thieves and vagrant ruffians shun this area like the plague!'

'Then your job is simple, Siew. Just the administrative routine.' The captain sat down.

'No, sir,' he said gloomily, 'there you are wrong. Its very security from smaller criminals makes this area a proper paradise for the big ones! Suppose you were a wealthy crook with many personal enemies. Where better than here could you pass a quiet holiday? Here no assassin would ever dare to attack you. Or suppose you were the boss of an influential smuggling-ring, or of a secret criminal league? In your own territory you'd have to be on your guard day and night against killers sent by rival organizations. But here you could walk about freely without any fear of being molested. Do you see my problem now, sir?'

'Not quite. Since all arrivals must register, why not send those questionable characters back where they came from?'

The captain shook his head.

'First, hundreds of our tourists are decent people, and most merchants come here on legitimate business. We can't possibly verify the antecedents of every one of them. Second, a considerable portion of the income of the local people is derived from the tourist traffic. If we clamped down on all travellers, they would avoid this place, and we have strict orders from the capital to keep on good terms with the population. "Benevolent Rule" is His Majesty's reign-name, as you know, sir. It's a ticklish situation, for no one can tell when trouble'll flare up among some of the big scoundrels on holiday here. And I am responsible for the maintenance of peace and order in Rivertown!'

'Quite true. But I can't see what I can do about it.'

'You might just have a look at the situation, sir! From the other side of the counter, so to speak. A man of your long experience and splendid record as a criminal investigator would . . .'

Judge Dee raised his hand.

'All right. I don't mind getting a first-hand impression of the problems presented by a Special Area. I . . .'

There was a knock and the lieutenant came back. He put two sheets before his chief. One was Judge Dee's own identity document. The captain concentrated his attention on the second, a slightly soiled piece of paper with frayed edges.

'Good!' he exclaimed with a broad smile. 'Very good indeed, Liu! Have a look at this, sir!' He pushed the second document over to the judge. It was an official identity paper issued four years before by the metropolitan authorities and made out to Dr. Liang Mou. The date of birth was Judge Dee's own, but the address was a well-known residential quarter in the capital.

'You notice the date, sir?' Captain Siew asked, rubbing his hands. 'The exact date on which the metropolitan authorities issued new papers to all citizens! Well done, Liu!' He took a seal from his drawer, stamped a corner of the paper, then wrote across it: 'Bearer is on his way back to the capital. Permitted to stay three days.' He added the date, and initialled it with a flourish of his brush.

'There you are, sir! All set! Your own paper I'll keep here under lock and key for you. Awkward if you were found to be carrying two different ones! I advise you to stay in the Kingfisher, sir; it's a nice quiet hostel, and most of the bigwigs lodge there.' Rising he added briskly, 'Needless to say, I am completely at your service, sir! Any time, day or night!'

Judge Dee got up too.

'To tell you the truth, Siew, when you mentioned your problem, I thought you were referring to the murder of the cashier of the Kingfisher. The man whose corpse you viewed on the quay.'

'Bad case, that! But the chap was murdered outside my territory, sir. Had it looked into at once. The night-watch spotted him leaving town an hour or so after midnight, going east. And my patrols haven't found any trace of robbers or highwaymen inside or near this area. Chap was murdered somewhere on the road to the mountains, and his body thrown into the river a couple of miles upstream. Got caught in the water-weeds opposite the ferry-house here. I'll be passing the case on to your colleague, the magistrate of our neighbouring district, to the east of Rivertown. Together with the stuff over there that we found in his sleeves.'

He took the judge to a side-table and pointed at a folded map, an abacus, a package of visiting-cards and a string of cash. Judge Dee casually unfolded the map and studied it for a while.

'It's a detailed map of the province,' he remarked. 'The road from Rivertown to Ten Miles Village, beyond the eastern mountain-ridge, is marked in red.'

THE CAPTAIN SHOWS JUDGE DEE A MAP

'Exactly! That's evidently where the chap was heading for, absconding with his employer's twenty silver pieces. That innkeeper is a notorious miser, you know. Fellow had the cheek to ask me to make good his loss! Please take this abacus and give it back to the old skinflint, sir. Wouldn't put it beyond him to accuse me of having stolen it!'

The judge put the counting-frame into his sleeve.

'I'll gladly do that. But you had better mention the thing in your report to my colleague. It might have a bearing on the case. It might mean, for instance, that the cashier was prepared for some complicated financial transaction in the village he was going to.'

The captain shrugged.

'An abacus goes with a cashier, sir. But I'll mention it anyway.'

While Judge Dee was strapping his sword to his back he asked:

'How do you know that the cashier wanted to steal the silver?'

'Old Wei stated that the youngster took the silver from the cash-box, sir. And you can trust Wei to know how much there was, to the very last copper! He runs the Kingfisher well, but he's a sour old codger. People say that his wife did wrong, of course, but they don't blame her too much. She eloped, you know, couple of weeks ago. Well, I am awfully grateful that you'll let me have your views on the situation, sir. But don't let it keep you from making a few fishing-trips up river! They have fine perch here. Trout too.'

He conducted the judge ceremoniously downstairs, and the burly lieutenant Liu opened the door. It was pouring with rain.

'Beastly weather, sir! Fortunately the Kingfisher is only a little way ahead—on your right. Good-night!'

# III

The judge quickly walked on, holding the oiled cloth over his head as protection against the downpour. The main street was deserted, for the hour of the evening rice was approaching. With a wry smile he reflected that Captain Siew had been much too glib. His story about the problem presented by unwanted visitors had been so much eyewash. And Siew wasn't interested in the murder of the cashier either. There must be another reason why Captain Siew wanted him to stay in Rivertown incognito. And a very cogent reason too, otherwise the captain wouldn't have made such elaborate arrangements to furnish him with a new identity. Siew was a shrewd customer, and observant too—he had spotted him at once on the quay, despite his dishevelled appearance.

Suddenly Judge Dee halted in his steps, oblivious of the rain. On the quay the captain had seemed rather slim, whereas Siew was a thick-set man. And on the quay he had got only a glimpse of the man's face, half-covered by his neckcloth. The judge creased his thick eyebrows. The lieutenant had expertly whisked him upstairs by a side-entrance, and nobody had seen him, the judge, enter or leave the captain's office. Now he was alone in a town he didn't know, and carrying faked papers. For one brief moment he had a premonition of trouble ahead. Then he shrugged. If there was any trickery about, he would know soon enough.

A large lampion was dangling from the eaves of a pillared portico, inscribed 'Inn of the Kingfisher'. Across the street he saw an even bigger one, bearing the inscription 'Inn of the Nine Clouds'. After a momentary hesitation he stepped onto the portico of the first. Having shaken out the wet oil-cloth, he entered the cavernous hall. It was lit by a tall brass candle that threw weird shadows on the plastered walls.

'All the large rooms are taken, sir,' the young clerk behind the

16

counter informed him. 'But we have a nice small back-room left on the second floor.'

'That will do,' Judge Dee said. While filling out the register with his new name and profession, he added, 'Before going up I want a bath and a change of clothes. When you have shown me the bathroom, you'll send a man to the blacksmith on the quay to fetch my saddle-bags.' As he pushed the register back over the counter, he felt the weight in his sleeve. He took the abacus out. 'When I registered at Headquarters, they asked me to return this counting-frame. It belonged to the cashier here, whose body was found in the river.'

The clerk thanked him and put the abacus in the drawer. 'When the boss saw our poor Tai on the quay,' he said with a sneer, 'he thought this thing was the package with his twenty silver pieces. Serves the old miser right!' He cast a quick glance over his shoulder at the high screen of lattice work. Behind it a man sat bent over a writing-desk. 'I'll lead the way, Doctor!'

The bath was located in the back of the inn. The dressing-room was empty, but the bundles of clothing lying about there and the raucous voices coming from behind the bamboo sliding-doors proved that other guests were using the pool. Judge Dee stepped out of his riding-boots and laid his sword, his wet cap and the calabash on the rack. He took the brocade folder with his money and his papers from his sleeve and put it under his cap, then stripped and opened the sliding-doors.

The shouting came from two naked men who were shadow-boxing in front of the large sunken pool. They were encouraging each other with bawdy remarks. Both were powerfully built and had the coarse faces of professional bullies. They fell silent at once when they saw the judge and gave him a sharp look.

'Go on boxing but keep your foul mouths shut!' a dry voice ordered. The speaker was a portly, middle-aged man who was sitting on the low bench by the side of the pool. The bath attendant standing behind him was vigorously kneading his flabby shoulders. As the two bullies resumed their exercise, Judge Dee squatted on the black-tiled floor and sluiced himself with the bucket of hot

**17**

water. Then he sat down on the bench, waiting for his turn to be scrubbed by the attendant.

'Where are you from, sir?' the elderly man by his side inquired politely.

'From the capital. My name is Liang; I am a doctor.' It would have been rude not to give a civil answer to a fellow bather. The bath is the only place in an inn where the guests meet socially.

The other surveyed Judge Dee's muscular arms and broad chest.

'You are a living advertisement for your medical skill, Doctor! My name is Lang Liu, from the south. Those two yokels are my assistants. I am . . . brr!' He broke off, for the attendant had sluiced him with cold water. He took a deep breath. 'I am a silk merchant, taking a holiday here. Hadn't counted on such infernal weather!'

They exchanged some remarks about the climate down south while the attendant scrubbed the judge clean. Then he stepped into the pool and stretched himself out in the hot water.

The elderly man had himself rubbed dry, then told the two boxers curtly, 'Get a move on!' They quickly dried themselves and meekly followed the portly man into the dressing-room.

Judge Dee thought that Lang didn't look like one of the wealthy crooks the captain had spoken about. He even had rather a distinguished appearance with his regular, haughty face and wispy goatee. And wealthy merchants often travelled with a bodyguard. The hot water was loosening up his stiff limbs, but now he realized that he was getting hungry. He got up and had the attendant vigorously rub him dry.

His two saddle-bags had been put ready in a corner of the dressing-room. Opening the first to get out a clean robe, he suddenly checked himself. His assistant Ma Joong, who always packed his bags for him, was a neat man; but these clothes were folded carelessly. He quickly opened the second bag. His night-robes, felt shoes and spare caps were all there, but this bag had also been tampered with. He quickly looked under his cap on the rack.

18

on, 'Well, since poor Tai is dead, there's no harm in telling you. The cashier was head over ears in love with my aunt, you see.'

'Your aunt? She must have been much older than he!'

'She was, about ten years, I think. But there never was anything between them, sir. He just adored her from a distance! And she didn't care for him, for she eloped with another man, as you may have heard.'

'Do you have any idea who that man was?'

She vigorously shook her small head.

'My aunt managed that affair very cleverly; I never even dreamt that she could be unfaithful to my uncle. When he told us that she had left him for another man I could hardly believe my ears. She had always seemed such a quiet, kind woman . . . much better than my Uncle Wei!' She gave him a quick, appraising look and added with a faint smile, 'You are a very nice man to talk to, sir! Perhaps it's because you are a doctor.'

The last remark unaccountably annoyed the judge. He asked the first question that came to mind:

'Since the cashier admired your aunt so much, her eloping with another man greatly distressed him, I suppose?'

'No, he wasn't sad at all.' She pensively patted her hair. 'Rather strange, if you come to think of it.'

Judge Dee raised his eyebrows.

'Are you quite sure? Those prolonged, purely sentimental attachments often affect a man more deeply than a brief, passionate affair.'

'Absolutely. Once I even caught him humming a song while he was doing the accounts.'

The judge picked up a morsel of salted vegetable, and slowly chewed it. Mrs Wei had effectively hoodwinked her young niece. The cashier had been her lover, of course. She had gone alone to the village across the mountains marked in red on the map found on Tai Min's dead body. They had agreed that the cashier would follow after a few weeks. But highwaymen had attacked him on the way and murdered him. Now his mistress must be waiting for him in Ten Miles Village, in vain. He would give these facts to Captain Siew, to be passed on to the magistrate in the neighbouring district. Everybody assumed that Tai had been murdered by robbers, but it might be much more complicated than that. 'Eh, what did you say?'

'I asked whether you were here to see a patient, sir.'

'No, I am just on a holiday. Planned to do some fishing. You must tell me where to go some time.'

'I'll do better than that! I can take you up river myself in our boat. Today I must help the maids, but tomorrow morning I'll be free.'

'That's awfully kind of you. Let's see how the weather turns out. By the way, what's your name?'

'I am called Fern, sir.'

'Well, Fern, I mustn't keep you from your duties. Thanks very much!'

He ate his dinner with gusto. When he had finished, he slowly drank a cup of strong tea, then leaned back in his chair, in a pleasant, relaxed mood. In the room below someone was playing a moon-guitar. The lilting melody, faintly heard, stressed the silence of the rest of the inn. The judge listened for a while to the melody that seemed vaguely familiar. When the music stopped he sat up.

He decided that his worries about Captain Siew and his motives must be ascribed to the fact that he was tired after the long ride through the forest. Why shouldn't the captain be genuinely interested in an outsider's views on the local situation? And as to the elaborate arrangement of his alias, well, he knew that secret service people always took delight in such details. He would be just as thorough himself now! With a smile he got up and went to the wall-table. Opening the lacquered box that contained writing material, he selected a sheet of good red paper, folded it, and tore it into six oblong pieces. He moistened the writing-brush and inscribed each of the improvised visiting-cards in large letters with his new name 'Doctor Liang Mou'. Having put those in his sleeve, he picked up his sword and his calabash and went downstairs. He felt like taking a look at the town.

In the hall Mr Wei was standing at the counter, talking in undertones with the clerk. The innkeeper quickly came to meet the judge. After having made a low bow he said in his hoarse voice:

'I am Wei Cheng, the owner of this inn, Doctor. There was a messenger here for you just now, sir. Since he didn't give his name, I told him to wait outside. I was just going to send my clerk up to tell you.'

Judge Dee smiled inwardly. This had to be a message from Captain Siew. He found his boots standing amongst the other footwear by the door, stepped into them and went out. Dressed in a black jacket and wide black trousers a tall man with crossed arms was leaning against a pillar. Both his jacket and his round cap had red borders.

'I am Doctor Liang. What can I do for you?'

'A sick person wants to consult you, Doctor,' the other replied curtly. 'Over there in the palankeen.'

Reflecting that the captain's message must be very secret indeed, the judge followed the man to the large, black-curtained palankeen a little farther down the street. The six bearers squatting with their backs against the wall rose at once. They wore the same dress as their foreman. Judge Dee drew the door-curtain aside. Then he stood stock still. He found himself face to face with a young woman. She wore a long black mantle with a black hood that set off the pallor of her comely but haughty face.

'I . . . I must inform you that I don't deal with women's diseases,' he muttered. 'Therefore I advise you to consult . . .'

'Step inside and I'll explain,' she cut him short. She moved over to make room for him. As soon as the judge had sat down on the narrow bench, the door-curtain was drawn close from the outside. The bearers lifted the shafts on their shoulders and went off at a quick trot.

## IV

'What does this nonsense mean?' Judge Dee asked coldly.

'It means that my mother wants to see you,' the girl snapped. 'Her name is Hydrangea; she is the Chief Lady-in-waiting of Her Highness.'

'Is your mother ill?'

'Wait till we are out in the forest.'

The judge decided to wait till he knew more about her mysterious errand before putting this forward young lady in her place. The bearers were slackening their pace. Now it was very still outside.

After about a quarter of an hour, the girl suddenly pulled the window-curtain open. They were moving along a forest road, lined by tall pine trees. The girl took off the hood with a careless gesture. Her hair was done up in a simple but elegant coiffure, with a gold filigreed comb in front. Her small, slightly uptilted nose gave her face a pert expression. Turning to the judge, she said in the same peremptory voice:

'I must tell you here and now that I don't know what all this is about! I am just following instructions. So you needn't bother me with questions.' She groped under the bench and came up with a flat box of red-lacquered pigskin, the sort that doctors use to carry their prescriptions. Putting it on her lap, she resumed, 'In this box you'll find a package of prescription blanks, a dozen of your name-cards, and . . .'

'I have prepared cards myself, thank you,' Judge Dee said curtly.

'Never mind. There are also some plasters and six folders containing a quite innocent powder. Have you ever been to the town of Wan-hsiang, eighty miles upriver?'

'I passed through there once.'

'Good. Behind the Temple of the War God lives the Honourable Kuo, retired secretary of the Palace Archives. He knew you from the capital, and he summoned you last week because he is suffering from asthma. Now you are on your way back to the capital. Can you remember all that?'

'I'll try,' the judge replied dryly.

'The Honourable Kuo wrote to my mother that you would be passing through here, so she had you called for a consultation. She suffers from asthma too, and yesterday she had a bad attack.' She darted a quick look at him and asked, annoyed, 'Why do you carry a sword? It'll make a bad impression. Put it under the bench!'

Judge Dee slowly unstrapped the sword. He knew that outsiders were not allowed to enter any palace armed.

After they had been carried along through the silent forest for some time, the road broadened. They passed under a double-arched stone portal of massive structure, then crossed a broad marble bridge with elaborately carved balustrades. On the other side of the moat loomed the high double-gate of the Water Palace. The girl pulled the window-curtain close. The judge heard shouted commands, and the palankeen stopped abruptly. The foreman of the bearers exchanged a few whispered words with the sentries; then they were carried up a flight of stairs. The grating sounds of bolts being drawn and chains released indicated that the gate was being thrown open. More shouted orders, and the palankeen was carried ahead for some distance, then lowered to the ground. The door- and window-curtains on both sides of the palankeen were drawn aside at the same moment. The glaring light that fell inside temporarily blinded Judge Dee's eyes. When he opened them he was looking at the face of a sergeant of the guard, close by the window. Behind him stood six guardsmen in their gilt armour, drawn swords in their hands. The sergeant told the girl curtly:

'You are all right, of course, miss.' And to the judge: 'State name, profession and purpose of visit!'

'I am Doctor Liang Mou, summoned by the Lady Hydrangea, Chief Lady-in-waiting of Her Imperial Highness.'

'Step down, please!'

Two guards searched the judge quickly and expertly. They even

25

felt in his boots and brought out his identity paper. The sergeant inspected it. 'All right. You'll get it back when you leave, sir. The doctor's box please, miss!' The sergeant opened the flat box and rummaged with his thick forefinger among the contents. Giving it to the judge, he held up his hand for the calabash. He uncorked it, shook it in order to verify there was no small dagger inside, then gave it back. 'You may now change to the palace chair.'

He barked an order. Four bearers in beautiful silk livery approached, carrying an elegant litter with gilt shafts and brocade curtains. After the judge and the young woman had stepped inside, it was born noiselessly across the marble-paved courtyard, the sergeant marching in front. The spacious court was brilliantly lit by countless silk lampions, each on a high, red-lacquered stand. A few dozen guardsmen were loitering there, all in full armour and carrying crossbows and quivers packed with long arrows. The next yard was quiet; courtiers in flowing blue robes were flitting about among the heavy pillars that lined the open corridors. Judge Dee pointed at the lotus ponds and murmuring water-conducts.

'All that water comes from the river, I suppose?'

'That's why it's called the Water Palace,' the girl snapped.

At a double-gate of gilt trellis work, two sentries carrying long halberds stopped the litter. The sergeant explained the purpose of the visit, then marched off. The sentries closed the curtains and fastened them on the outside. The two occupants were sitting in the dark again.

'Outsiders are not allowed to see the layout of the inner palace,' the girl deigned to explain.

The judge remembered that on the map in Captain Siew's office the Water Palace was represented by a blank square. The authorities were nothing if not thorough in their security measures. He tried to guess what course they were following but soon lost count of all the corners they turned, all the steps they were carried up and down. At last the litter was lowered to the ground. A giant in heavy armour and a spiked helmet decorated with long coloured plumes told them to descend. His colossal colleague knocked with

26

the hilt of his naked broadsword on a double-door of tooled iron. The judge got a glimpse of a paved yard, surrounded by a high wall painted a bright purple; then the iron doors swung open and a fat man motioned them to enter. He was clad in a long, gold-embroidered robe, and wore a conical, black-lacquered hat. His round placid face with its broad fleshy nose was completely hairless. Nodding familiarly at the girl, the obese eunuch addressed the judge in a high reedy voice:

'His Excellency the Chief Eunuch wants to see you before you cross the Golden Bridge, Doctor.'

'My mother is in distress,' the girl quickly intervened. 'The doctor must see her immediately, for . . .'

'His Excellency's orders were explicit,' the moon-faced man told her placidly. 'You'll kindly wait here, miss. This way, sir.' He pointed down a long, silent passage.

# V

Alarmed, Judge Dee realized that he had barely half a minute to decide. It would take only that long to reach the gold-lacquered door at the end of the passage.

Up to now he had not been concerned about the irregularity of the situation, for the person who had summoned him in this unusual manner had to be someone of consequence, and fully aware of his true identity, duly reported by the wily Captain Siew. That person wished to keep the real purpose of his visit secret, and would assume full responsibility for his having entered the palace under false pretences. But evidently his unknown sponsor had not reckoned with the Chief Eunuch interfering. During the coming interview the judge would either have to lie to one of the highest Court officials, which went against his deepest convictions of his duties to the State, or tell the truth, the consequences of which move he couldn't even guess at. The truth might harm a good cause, but also, perhaps, thwart an evil scheme. He took hold of himself. If a corrupt courtier or a depraved official was intending to use him for a nefarious purpose, it meant that he, the judge, had somewhere fallen short of the ideals of honesty and justice he wanted to live by, and hence fully deserved the ignominious death awaiting him if his true identity were discovered. This reflection gave him back his inner certainty. While the obese eunuch was knocking at the door, Judge Dee groped in his sleeve for one of the red visiting-cards he had written in the Kingfisher.

He knelt down just inside the door, respectfully raising the card with both hands above his bent head. Someone took the card and he heard a brief, whispered conversation. Then a thin voice spoke petulantly:

'Yes, yes, I know all that! Let me see your face, Doctor Liang!'

As the judge raised his head he saw with surprise that instead

28

of the sumptuous office he had expected, he found himself in what seemed the elegant library of a scholar of fastidious taste. To the right and left stood high bookcases, loaded with brocade-bound volumes and manuscript rolls, and the wide window at the back opened onto a charming garden where a profusion of flowers blossomed among quaintly shaped rocks. On the broad windowsill stood a row of orchids, in coloured bowls of exquisite porcelain. Their subtle fragrance pervaded the quiet room. Beside the rosewood desk an old man was sitting hunched in an enormous armchair of carved ebony. He was enveloped in a wide robe of shimmering stiff brocade that sloped down from his narrow shoulders like a tent. The sallow face, with thin grey moustache and wispy chinbeard, seemed small and pinched under the high tiara, lavishly decorated with gold filigree set with glittering jewels. Behind the armchair stood a tall, broad-shouldered man dressed entirely in black. With impassive face he let a red silk noose glide through his large, hairy hands. For a while the old man looked the judge over with heavy-lidded, vacant eyes. Then he said:

'Rise and come nearer!'

The judge hastily came to his feet and advanced three steps. He made a low bow, then raised his hands in his folded sleeves, waiting for the Chief Eunuch to address him. The sound of heavy breathing told him that the obese eunuch was standing close behind him.

'Why should the Lady Hydrangea have summoned you?' the old man asked in his querulous voice. 'We have four excellent physicians on our staff.'

'This person,' Judge Dee replied respectfully, 'could, of course, never dare to compete with the great doctors attached to the palace. It so happened, however, that by a mere stroke of good luck I succeeded in alleviating similar symptoms the Honourable Kuo suffered from. In his great kindness, the Honourable Kuo must have given the Lady Hydrangea a much exaggerated impression of this person's poor skill.'

'I see.' The Chief Eunuch slowly rubbed his bony chin, moodily surveying the judge. Suddenly he looked up and ordered crisply:

'Leave us alone!' The man in black went to the door, followed by the obese eunuch. As the door closed behind them, the old man slowly got up from the armchair. If it hadn't been for his bent shoulders he would have been nearly as tall as the judge. He said in a tired voice:

'I want to show you my flowers. Come here!' He shuffled to the window. 'This white orchid is a rare specimen, and most difficult to raise. It has a delicate, elusive fragrance.' As Judge Dee bent over the flower, the old eunuch went on, 'I look after it personally, every day. To give and nourish life, Doctor, is not entirely denied to persons of my status.'

The judge righted himself.

'The process of creation is indeed a universal one, Excellency. Those who think it is man's monopoly are very foolish indeed.'

'It's a relief,' the other said, a little wistfully, 'to have a talk with an intelligent man in private. There are too many eyes and ears in a palace, Doctor. Far too many.' Then, with a nearly shy look in his hooded eyes, he asked, 'Tell me, why did you choose the medical profession?'

The judge considered for a while. The question could be interpreted in two ways. He decided to play it safe.

'Our ancient sages say, Excellency, that illness and suffering are but deviations from the Universal Way. I thought it would be rewarding to try returning those deviations to their natural course.'

'You'll have found out that failure is as frequent as success.'

'I have resigned myself to the limitations of human endeavour, Excellency.'

'The correct attitude, Doctor. Very correct.' He clapped his hands. When the obese eunuch had reappeared, the old man told him, 'Doctor Liang is permitted to cross the Golden Bridge.' He added to the judge in a dull voice, 'I trust that this one visit will suffice. We are greatly concerned about the health of the Lady Hydrangea, but we can't have people from outside going in and out of here all the time. Good-bye.'

Judge Dee made a very low bow. The Chief Eunuch sat down at his desk and bent over his papers.

30

The fat eunuch took the judge down the corridor where the young woman was waiting. He told her unctuously, 'You are permitted to take the doctor across, miss.' She turned round and walked on without deigning to reply.

The long passage ended in a round moon-door, guarded by two tall sentries. At a sign from the fat man they opened it and the three stepped down into a beautifully laid-out garden of flowering trees, bisected by a narrow canal. A curved marble bridge only three feet broad led across it. The elaborately carved balustrade was encrusted with gold. On the other side rose a high purple wall with only one small gate. Above it the curved, yellow-tiled roofs of a detached palace were just visible. The eunuch halted at the foot of the bridge. 'I'll be waiting for you here, Doctor!'

'Wait till you weigh an ounce, fathead!' the young woman snapped. 'But don't dare to put one of your flat feet on the bridge!'

As she was taking the judge across, he realized that he was now entering the strictly forbidden area, the abode of the Third Princess.

Two court ladies admitted them to a spacious courtyard where a number of young women were loitering under waving willow trees. When this bevy of beauties saw the newcomers, they began to whisper excitedly, the jewelled hair-dos of their bobbing heads glittering in the moonlight. Judge Dee's guide led him through a small side-door into a bamboo garden, and on to the open verandah at the back. A sedate matron was preparing tea at a side-table. She made a bow and whispered to the young girl, 'Her Ladyship had a bad coughing attack just now.'

The girl nodded and took the judge into a luxuriously appointed bedroom. As she bolted the door, Judge Dee bestowed a curious look upon the enormous bedstead that took up the greater part of the back wall. In front, close to the brocade bed-curtains, a high tabouret stood ready, a small cushion on its round top.

'Doctor Liang has arrived, Mother,' the young woman announced.

The bed-curtains were parted just an inch, and a wrinkled hand appeared. A bracelet of pure white jade, carved into the shape of a curving dragon, encircled the thin wrist. The girl placed the hand on the cushion, then went to stand by the bolted door.

Judge Dee put his box on the tabouret and felt the pulse with the tip of his forefinger. (Doctors are not allowed to see more of a distinguished lady-patient than her hand, and must diagnose the illness from the condition of the pulse.) Suddenly the woman behind the curtains told him in a hurried whisper:

'Go through the panel on the left of this bedstead. Quick!'

Astonished, the judge let go of her wrist and went round the bed. Set in the dark wainscot were three high panels. As soon as he pressed against the one nearest to the bed, it swung inside noiselessly. He stepped into an ante-room, lit by a high floor-lamp of white silk. Under the lamp a lady was sitting in the corner of a massive ebony couch. She was reading a book. The judge dropped to his knees, for he had seen the long-sleeved jacket of the Imperial yellow brocade. They were alone in the still room. The only sound heard was the faint crackling of the sandalwood log in the antique bronze burner standing in front of the couch. The blue smoke perfumed the room with a fleeting sweet smell.

The lady looked up from her book and said in a clear, melodious voice:

'Rise, Dee. Since time is short, you are allowed to forgo all empty formality.' She put the limp volume down on the couch and surveyed him with her large, troubled eyes. He took a deep breath. She was indeed one of the loveliest women he had ever seen. Her pale face was a perfect oval, framed by the glossy mass of her elaborate high coiffure that was fixed by two long hair-needles with knobs of translucent green jade. Thin eyebrows crossed her smooth high forehead in two long curves, and the small mouth was cherry-red under the finely chiselled nose. There was a great dignity about her, yet at the same time the natural ease of a warm unaffected personality. She resumed slowly:

'I summoned you, Dee, because I was told that you are a great investigator, and our loyal servant. I did so in this unusual manner because the inquiry I shall order you to conduct must be kept secret. Two days ago, towards midnight, I was in the pavilion built on the outer wall overlooking the river. Alone.' She cast a forlorn look at the silvery paper of the high lattice window. 'A

THE THIRD PRINCESS GRANTS AN AUDIENCE

brilliant moon was in the sky, just as tonight, and I went to stand at the window, to enjoy the view. First, however, I took off my necklace and laid it on the tea-table, to the left of the entrance. That necklace, Dee, is an Imperial treasure. It consists of eighty-four unusually large, perfectly matched pearls. Father gave it to Mother, and after Mother had died, the necklace was conferred upon me.'

The Third Princess paused. Looking with downcast eyes at the long white hands clasped in her lap, she went on:

'I took the necklace off because I once lost an ear-ring leaning out of that same window. I don't know how long I stood there, absorbed in the charming river scene. When at last I turned round to go back inside, the necklace was gone.'

She lifted her long-lashed eyes and looked straight at the judge.

'I ordered the palace authorities to institute a most thorough search, at once. Both in and outside my palace. As yet they haven't found the slightest clue. And the day after tomorrow I have to return to the capital. I must have the necklace back by then, for Father wants to see me wearing it, always. I think . . . no, I am convinced that the theft was committed by an outsider, Dee. He must have come in a boat and scaled the wall, taking the necklace while I was standing there with my back to him. The movements of every single person in this section of my palace were checked thoroughly. Therefore the thief must be someone outside the palace, and therefore I put you in charge of the investigation, Dee.

'You shall search for the necklace in the utmost secrecy; no one in or outside the palace shall know that I entrusted this task to you. As soon as you have found it, however, you shall abandon your incognito, proceed here in your official capacity and publicly restore the necklace to me. Rip the seam of your collar open, Dee.'

While the judge pulled the seam of the right lapel of his robe apart, she took from her sleeve a tightly folded piece of yellow paper. Rising, she pushed the paper into the lining of his robe. She was tall; her coiffure brushed his face and he perceived its subtle fragrance. She sat down again and resumed:

'The paper I have just given you will enable you to enter the

34

palace openly, without anyone daring to interfere. You shall return it to me together with my necklace.' Her beautiful lips curved in a slow smile as she added, 'I place my happiness in your hands, Dee.'

She nodded in dismissal and took up her book again.

# VI

Judge Dee made a low bow, and stepped back into the room of the Lady-in-waiting. The panel closed noiselessly behind him. The Lady Hydrangea's white hand still reposed on the small cushion. As he felt her wrist again, there was a knock on the door. Her daughter pulled the bolt back without making any noise, and admitted two court ladies. The first bore a tray of writing implements, the other a bamboo basket with a clean night-robe.

The judge let go of the slender wrist, opened his flat box and took a prescription blank. He beckoned the first court lady, selected a brush from her tray and rapidly jotted down his prescription: a mild dose of ephedrine and a sedative. 'Have this medicine prepared at once,' he told Hydrangea's daughter. 'I trust this will greatly relieve the patient.' He snapped the box closed and went to the door. The young woman silently took him across the court-yard and to the bridge, then left without so much as saying good-bye.

On the other side the obese eunuch was waiting for him. 'You were only a short time, Doctor,' he said with satisfaction. He conducted the judge through the many corridors of the Chief Eunuch's residence to the main entrance, where the litter was standing ready.

Leaning back against the soft upholstery, Judge Dee went over the amazing interview in his mind. The Princess had given him the bare facts, nothing more. Evidently the background of this amazing theft had to do with delicate matters which she could not or would not explain in detail. But he had the distinct feeling that what she had left unsaid was much more important than the facts of the case. She was convinced that the theft had been committed by an outsider, but the thief had obviously had an accomplice inside the palace. For he must have known in advance that the Princess would be in the pavilion at that particular hour, then been informed in some way that she had taken off her pearl necklace and placed it on the corner-table. Only a man watching her from a secret coign of vantage in that section of the palace could have seen her, and given a sign to warn the thief waiting in a small boat under the pavilion.

The judge frowned. At first sight it seemed a most risky and unnecessarily complicated scheme. Even if the Princess really was in the habit of standing at the pavilion window around midnight, she would surely be accompanied by one or more of her court ladies most of the time. And the organizers of the theft could hardly have had a boat moored under the pavilion every night there was a brilliant moon! One would have to assume that the ramparts of the palace were manned by guards day and night, and they would soon spot any boat lying there. The more he thought about it, the less he liked it. It all seemed very far-fetched. The only point that was clear was why she had chosen him to help: she suspected a particular person in her closest retinue of being concerned in the theft, therefore she needed an investigator who had no connections in the palace and whom nobody in the palace knew to be engaged in the search for the necklace. Hence her insisting on the utmost secrecy. It was a pity she had not given him a general idea of the lay-out of her section of the palace. His first task was evidently to have a look at the north wall from the river, and study the location of the pavilion and the surrounding area.

He sighed. Well, he need not worry any more about his having entered the palace under false pretences, or about having lied to the Chief Eunuch. The document concealed in the lining of his collar would doubtless state clearly that he was acting on the express orders of the Third Princess. Nor was there any need to worry about Captain Siew's motives any more. That sly fellow must have known about the theft, probably through his chief, Colonel Kang, who, as commanding officer of the Imperial Guard, must have taken part in the investigation. And Siew had recommended him, the judge, as a suitable person to conduct a secret inquiry all by himself. He smiled wryly. The rascal had hoodwinked him good and proper!

The litter was lowered and the door-curtain pulled aside. They were in the courtyard where he and Hydrangea's daughter had changed palankeens. A lieutenant of the guard told him gruffly:

'Follow me. I have orders to take you to His Excellency the Superintendent.'

Judge Dee bit his lip. If he were found out now, he would be betraying the confidence of the Princess before he had even begun the task entrusted to him. He was ushered into a lofty hall. Behind the ornamental desk in the centre, piled with papers, sat a thin man with an austere face, a grey moustache and stringy chinbeard stressing his ascetic look. His winged brown cap had golden rims, and his square shoulders were encased in a robe of stiff brown brocade. He seemed engrossed in the document before him. A portly courtier wearing the blue robe and cap of a councillor stood behind his chair, reading over his shoulder. In front of the desk were gathered about a dozen courtiers. Some carried document boxes, others bulky dossiers. When the judge bent his head and raised his hands in a respectful salutation, he felt their eyes boring into his back.

'Doctor Liang has arrived, Excellency,' the lieutenant reported.

The Superintendent looked up. As he leaned back in his chair, the judge cast a quick look at the document the Superintendent and the councillor had been studying so intently. His heart sank. It was his own identity paper. Fixing the judge with his small piercing eyes, the Superintendent asked in a crisp, metallic voice:

'How is the Lady Hydrangea?'

'I prescribed a medicine for her, Excellency. I trust her ladyship will make a speedy recovery.'

'Where did the consultation take place?'

'I suppose it was in her ladyship's bedroom, Excellency. Her daughter was present, and also two court ladies.'

'I see. I hope that the medicine you prescribed will prove effective, Doctor. In the first place for her, of course. But also for you. Since you have taken over the treatment, from now on you will be held responsible for her, Doctor.' He pushed the identity paper over to Judge Dee. 'You shan't leave Rivertown until you have obtained my permission. You may go.'

38

The lieutenant took Judge Dee outside. When they were half-way across the yard, the lieutenant suddenly halted and saluted sharply. A very tall officer strode past in the gold-plated armour and plumed helmet of a colonel of the guard, his iron boots clanking on the marble slabs. The judge got a brief glimpse of a pale, handsome face, with a jet-black moustache and a clipped chin-beard.

'Was that Colonel Kang?' he asked the lieutenant.

'Yes, sir.' He led the judge to the first courtyard where the same black palankeen that had fetched him from the Kingfisher stood ready. He stepped inside and was carried out through the high gates.

When they had crossed the broad marble bridge over the moat, Judge Dee pulled the window-curtain aside to let the evening air cool his flushed face. It had been a tremendous relief that his faked paper had passed muster. But how must he interpret the suspicious attitudes of, first, the Chief Eunuch and, just now, the Super-intendent? Did these high officials always adopt such a hostile manner towards strangers visiting the palace? Or were they perhaps implicated in the theft of the necklace? No, he was letting his imagination run away with him! Of course it was out of the question that high-ranking officials of the Imperial Court would stoop to connive at a theft! Money meant nothing to them, why should they risk. . . . Suddenly the judge sat up straight. Could it be that the pearl necklace was the gage in some complicated court intrigue, some subtle power struggle between opposing court cliques? That would explain why the Princess had kept the pur-pose of his visit secret from even her two closest servants, the Chief Eunuch and the Superintendent. On the other hand, if one or both had a special interest in the necklace, and suspected that he had met the Princess and been informed of the theft, why had they let him go without a really thorough questioning? To that question there was an obvious answer. They had only let him go because they didn't dare to oppose the Princess openly. They planned to have him eliminated outside, in a manner that could be conveniently explained as an accident. He felt under the bench. His sword was gone.

At the moment he made this unpleasant discovery, the palankeen was lowered to the ground. A tall man in black pulled the door-curtain aside.

'Please descend here, sir. Just follow this road, and you'll be in town in a few minutes.'

It was not the same foreman who had come to fetch him. Judge Dee stepped down and quickly looked around. They seemed to be in the middle of the pine forest. The bearers stared at him with impassive faces.

'Since the town is so near,' he told the foreman curtly, 'you had better carry me to my inn. I am tired.' He moved to re-enter the palankeen; but the foreman barred his way.

'I am very sorry, sir, but I have my orders.' The bearers lifted the palankeen on their shoulders, turned it round quickly and trotted back the way they had come, their foreman bringing up the rear. The judge was all alone among the tall, silent pines.

## VII

Judge Dee remained standing there for a while, pensively tugging at his long sidewhiskers. Serious trouble lay ahead, and there was very little he could do about it—except leave the road and try to get lost in the wood. But that wouldn't be much help either, for if assassins had been sent after him, they would be picked men thoroughly familiar with the terrain, and by now they would have thrown a cordon round this part of the forest. He decided to try to discover first whether his fears were well founded. There was a slight chance that the bearers were acting on the orders of the Lady Hydrangea, who for some reason or other didn't want him to be seen being carried back to town openly in a palace palankeen. And the sergeant at the gate might have inspected the palankeen, found his sword under the bench and confiscated it. He must do something to get it back, for it was a famous blade, made long ago by a great swordsmith, an heirloom treasured in his family for many generations. He pushed his flat box into the bosom of his robe and went ahead slowly in the shadow of the trees, keeping to the side of the road. There was no use in presenting a target to an ambitious archer.

At regular intervals he halted and listened. There was no sign of anyone following him, but nor could he hear the faintest sound to indicate he was in the vicinity of the town. Just when he was about to turn a bend he heard a strange, snorting noise ahead.

Quickly he ducked into the undergrowth and listened again. Now a twig snapped, a little further on. Carefully parting the branches, he worked his way through the shrubs until he saw a large, dark shape hovering among the pines. It was an old donkey grazing among the weeds.

As the judge went up to it, he saw a pair of crutches leaning against the gnarled stem of a colossal tree by the roadside. Underneath it Master Gourd was sitting hunched on a moss-covered

41

boulder. He still wore his patched brown robe, but his grey head was bare, the topknot covered by a piece of black cloth, the traditional headwear of the Taoist recluse. His calabash was standing at his feet. The old man looked up.

'You are up and about at a late hour, Doctor.'

'I went for a walk to enjoy the cool air. I must have got lost.'

'Where's your sword?'

'I was told it was perfectly safe to go about unarmed here.'

Master Gourd sniffed.

'I thought you'd have learned not to believe everything people say. As a doctor.' He groped behind him for his crutches. 'All right, I shall be your guide again. Come along, you won't have any trouble keeping pace with this ancient mount.' He tied the calabash to his belt, and climbed on the donkey.

Judge Dee felt relieved. With a well-known figure as Master Gourd as witness, the enemy wouldn't risk an open attack. After they had been going along for a while, he said with a faint smile:

'When I met you this afternoon in the woods on the other side of the town, you gave me something of a shock, you know! My eyes were sore, and the light bad. For one brief moment I thought I was seeing my double.'

Master Gourd reined in his donkey.

'Don't speak lightly of grave matters,' he said reprovingly. 'Nobody is one; all of us are an aggregate of many. But we conveniently forget our less satisfactory component parts. If one of those should manage to slip away from you, and you would meet it, you'd take it for a ghost, Doctor. And a very offensive ghost too!' He paused and listened. 'Talking about ghosts, don't you think we are being followed?'

Now Judge Dee, too, heard something moving about in the undergrowth. Quickly grabbing one of the crutches, he whispered:

'If we are attacked, you just clear out. I can look after myself; I am a stickfighter. Don't worry!'

'I am not worried, for nobody can harm me. I am just an empty shell, Doctor. Have been for many a year.'

Three men jumped out onto the road. They wore coarse jackets and trousers and their hair was bound up with red rags. All three

42

THE SECOND MEETING WITH MASTER GOURD

had swords, and two brandished short pikes. While one of them grabbed the donkey's reins, another raised his pike and barked at the judge:

'Better behave, bastard!'

Judge Dee was about to lunge with the crutch when suddenly he felt a sharp pain in the small of his back.

'Don't do that, dogshead!' a voice growled behind him.

'Put my crutch back, Doctor,' Master Gourd said. 'I need them both.'

'What do we do with the old geezer, boss?' the pike-wielder asked.

The man behind the judge cursed. 'Take him along too. It's just his bad luck.' Again the judge felt the point of the sword in his back. 'Walk on, you!'

The Judge decided that he couldn't do anything, for the moment. The scoundrels were paid assassins rather than ordinary robbers, and he was sure he could handle their kind. He walked on, saying only, 'I hope we won't meet a patrol. For your sakes, I mean.'

The man behind him guffawed.

'The soldiers have other things to worry about right now, you fool!'

The ruffians drove their prisoners along a narrow side-path. One led Master Gourd's donkey by the reins, a second followed with a pike, while the two others walked behind Judge Dee.

The path led to a clearing. A low brick building stood among the trees. They went to the second building that looked like a deserted godown. The man in front let go of the donkey's reins, kicked the door open and went inside. Soon a cone of light appeared. 'Get along!' One of the men behind the judge drove him inside, prodding him with his sword.

The godown was empty but for a few bales piled up in a corner and a wooden bench in front of some pillars to the right. The light came from a candle in a niche in the wall. The judge turned round and saw now the leader of the ruffians. He was a hulking man as tall as himself, with a coarse face framed by a stubbly ring-beard. He carried a long sword. The two others, one wielding a

44

pike and the second a sword, were mean-looking, powerfully built fellows. The judge went slowly to the centre of the room, watching for a chance to wrench a weapon from his captors. But they were evidently experienced men, for they kept him at a safe distance, their arms at the ready.

Master Gourd came hobbling inside, followed by the second pike-wielder. The old man made straight for the bench and sat down. Putting his crutches between his knees, he told the judge:

'Have a seat too, Doctor! You might as well be comfortable.'

Judge Dee sat down. If he made it look as if he had given up, he would stand a better chance of catching his enemies off guard. The leader was standing in front of the judge and Master Gourd; two others had taken up positions to the right and left of the bench; the fourth was standing behind Judge Dee, his sword ready. Testing the point of his sword with his thumb, the bearded leader said earnestly:

'Me and my friends want you to know that we have nothing against you two. We do what we are paid to do, because that's the only way we can make our living.'

The judge knew that this was the death sentence. Low-class scoundrels were superstitious; they always said this before killing their man, so as to prevent his ghost from haunting them afterwards and bringing them bad luck.

'We quite understand that,' Master Gourd said quietly. Then he lifted one of his crutches and pointed it at the leader with a trembling hand. 'What I don't understand is why they chose an ugly brute like you for the job!'

'I'll make you shut up, old wreck!' the bearded man shouted angrily.

He stepped up to Master Gourd. 'First I'll . . .'

At that moment the crutch suddenly became steady; it shot out, and its point bored deep into the bearded man's left eye. With a howl of pain he let his sword drop. Judge Dee dived to the floor and grabbed it, the weapon of the man behind him grazing his shoulder. The judge was on his feet in a second. He turned round and drove his sword into the breast of the other, who was about to stab Master Gourd from behind. Pulling the

45

sword out of his opponent's sagging body, the judge saw the
bearded leader rush at Master Gourd, cursing obscenely. Judge
Dee just had time to see Master Gourd's crutch shoot out again
with lightning speed and land right in the giant's midriff, when
he had to jump back and parry the blow the second swordsman
aimed at his head. There was one pike-wielder left. He raised his
weapon to throw it at the judge, but Master Gourd hooked the
crooked end of his crutch round the man's ankle. He toppled to
the floor, dropping his pike, which the old man drew towards
him with a deft movement of the crutch. The bearded giant was
rolling on the floor, clutching his stomach and emitting strangled
sounds.

The judge found that his opponent was an experienced swordsman. He had to do his very best to counter the man's confident
attack. The judge's borrowed sword lacked the fine balance of his
own weapon, the great blade 'Rain Dragon', but as soon as he had
become accustomed to it he drove his opponent back into a position from where he himself could keep an eye on the other two
ruffians. For the moment, however, he had to concentrate on his
own fight, for his opponent was executing a series of clever feints,
alternated with dangerous thrusts.

When the judge had gained the advantage again, he cast a
quick look at Master Gourd. The old man was still sitting on the
bench, but now he had a sword in his hand. He was parrying the
thrusts of his attacker with astonishing skill. The bearded giant
was staggering to his feet, trying to support himself against the
wall. Judge Dee's opponent was quick to utilize the moment of
inattention. He penetrated Judge Dee's guard with a long thrust to
the chest. Before the judge could side-step, the point of the sword
grazed his forearm. It would have pierced his side, but the flat
leather box which the judge had stuffed into his robe caught the
blow and saved his life.

The judge stepped back, his sword shot out, and with a series
of swift feints he succeeded in regaining the offensive. But blood
was trickling down from the wound in his forearm, and his lack
of training began to make him short of breath. Now he would
have to finish off his opponent as quickly as possible.

Lightning-quick, he shifted his sword from his right hand to his left. Like all superior swordsmen he was ambidextrous. Momentarily confused by the new angle of the attack, his opponent dropped his guard and the judge planted his sword in his throat. As the man fell backwards, Judge Dee rushed to help Master Gourd, shouting at the attacking swordsman to turn and defend himself. But suddenly the judge froze. Dumbfounded, he stared at what was an amazing spectacle.

The swordsman was leaping furiously about the seated man, showering him with lightning thrusts. But Master Gourd, leaning with his back against the pillar, parried every blow accurately, in a relaxed, unhurried manner. Whether the attack was aimed at his head or his feet, the old man's sword was always there just in time. Suddenly he lowered his sword, gripping the hilt with both hands. As his attacker lunged at him, he brought the sword up again, holding the hilt against the bench between his knees. The man could not check himself. As he fell forward, the old man's sword buried itself deep in his midriff.

The judge turned round. The bearded leader was coming for him, a crazed look in his one remaining eye. He had picked up a pike, and now aimed a sweeping thrust at Judge Dee's head. The judge ducked and drove his sword up into the other's breast. As the bearded leader sank to the floor, the judge bent over him and barked:

'Who sent you?'

The giant looked up at the judge with his one rolling eye. His thick lips twitched.

'How . . .' he began. A stream of blood came gushing from his mouth, his huge body was shaken by a convulsive shudder, and then he lay still. Judge Dee righted himself. Wiping his streaming face, he turned to Master Gourd and said panting:

'Thanks very much! That brilliant first move of yours put their leader out of action and saved the day!'

Master Gourd threw the sword into the corner. 'I hate weapons.'

'But you handle them with amazing skill! You met your opponent's thrusts so accurately, it seemed as if the points of your swords were joined by an invisible chain!'

47

'I told you I am only an empty shell,' the old man said testily. 'Being empty, my opponent's fullness flows automatically over into me. I become him, so I do exactly as he does. Fencing with me is like fencing with your own reflection in a mirror. And as pointless. Come over here; your arm is bleeding. A sick doctor is a sorry sight.'

The old man tore a piece of cloth from the dead giant's robe. Having expertly bandaged Judge Dee's forearm, he said, 'Better have a look outside, Doctor. See where we are, and whether our late lamented friends were expecting anyone!'

The judge went outside, his sword ready.

The donkey was grazing peacefully in the clearing, bleak in the pale moonlight. There was no one about. When he had inspected the building opposite, he found there were other godowns behind it. Having rounded the corner of the last one in the row, he saw the river before him. They were at the extreme east end of the quay. Slinging his sword, he walked back.

About to enter the godown, his eye fell on the inscription over the door: 'Property of Lang's Silk Firm'.

Pensively he smoothed his long beard. His bathroom acquaintance owned a silk shop in Rivertown. Since Lang was not a common name, the godown must belong to that inquisitive gentleman. Master Gourd came hobbling outside on his crutches.

'We are at the end of the quay,' Judge Dee told him. 'The whole place is deserted.'

'I'll go home, Doctor. I am tired.'

'Please pass by the blacksmith at the corner of the fish-market, sir. Ask him to send a man with my horse. I'll have another look at the dead men; then I'll have to report the attack to Headquarters.'

'Good. If anyone there wants my testimony, they know where to find me.' The old man climbed on his donkey and rode off.

Judge Dee went inside. The raw smell of the blood and the sight of the four dead men made him feel sick. Before searching them, he had a closer look at the bales in the corner. He slit one open with the point of his sword and found it did indeed contain raw silk. Then his eye was caught by dark stains on the bench he

48

and Master Gourd had been sitting on. The stains looked uncommonly like blood, spilt not so long ago. Under the bench he found a few thin ropes, also caked with dried blood. Then he turned to the dead men and searched their clothes. None of them had been carrying anything but a few coppers. He took the candle from the niche and scrutinized their faces. They looked like city hoodlums rather than highwaymen. Professional killers, efficient and probably well paid. By whom? Putting the candle back, he remembered the paper the Princess had given him. With index and middle finger he wormed the document from the lining of his collar. Unfolding it under the candle, he sucked in his breath. At the top of the document appeared the Emperor's personal seal, of vermilion colour and three inches square. Underneath was written in chancery hand that the bearer was temporarily appointed Imperial Inquisitor, vested with full executive powers. The date and Judge Dee's own name were added in the small elegant calligraphy of a lady. Below was the seal of the President of the Grand Council, and in a corner the personal seal of the Third Princess.

He folded the document carefully and put it back in the lining. That the Emperor had entrusted his daughter with an open edict of such tremendous import was eloquent proof of his unlimited trust and affection. It also constituted further proof that there was far more at stake than the theft of an Imperial treasure. The judge went outside, sat down on a tree-trunk and began to think things out.

# VIII

The neighing of a horse roused Judge Dee from his reverie. The groom dismounted, and the judge gave him a tip. Then he swung himself into the saddle, and rode down the quay.

At the fish-market he saw many people crowding round the street-stalls. Passing them, he caught a few words about a fire somewhere.

Outside the headquarters of the Guard a dozen or so mounted guardsmen had assembled. They were carrying storm-lanterns smeared with soot. Judge Dee handed his horse to a sentry and told him he wanted to see Lieutenant Liu. A soldier took him up the main staircase to Captain Siew's office. The captain sat behind his desk, talking to his burly lieutenant. He jumped up when he saw the judge and called out jovially:

'Glad you dropped in, sir! We had a busy night here. Roof of the City Granary caught fire, no one knows how. But my men had it under control soon. Take a seat, sir! You may go, Liu.'

Judge Dee sat down heavily.

'I want information on one of my fellow-guests in the King-fisher,' he said curtly. 'Fellow called Lang Liu.'

'So you set to work at once! I am most grateful, sir! Yes, Mr Lang is exactly the type of scoundrel I expected trouble from. He is the boss of all the brothel-keepers and gambling-houses in the southern part of this province, you see. Has organized them into a kind of secret guild, the Blue League it's called. Lang also owns a large silk firm down south, but that's just to give him a respectable front. As a rule he keeps within the limits of the law, and he's a very punctual tax-payer. Until very recently he had a lot of trouble with a rival, the so-called Red League, which manages the gambling and brothels in the neighbouring province.' He scratched his nose. 'I have heard it said that Mr Lang met representatives of the Red League here in Rivertown about ten days ago, and they agreed upon a kind of truce. Mr Lang must have decided to stay on here a little longer, just to observe how the truce would work out, from a safe distance! Remarkable how quickly you got on to him, sir!'

'He got on to me, rather.' The judge told Siew of his meeting with Lang in the bath, then he described the attack in the forest, saying that he had gone there for a walk and met Master Gourd. 'It was a well-planned attack,' he concluded. 'The fire in the Granary you mentioned was doubtless meant to keep your patrols busy at the other end of the town.'

'Holy heaven! The scoundrels! I am most awfully sorry this happened, sir. And right in my area! I don't like this at all!'

'I didn't like it either,' Judge Dee remarked dryly. 'At first we seemed to be at their mercy, but Master Gourd saved the situation. A most remarkable man. You know anything about his antecedents?'

'Not much, sir. He belongs to Rivertown, so to speak. Everybody knows him, but nobody knows where he came from. It's generally assumed that in his younger days he was a "brother of the green woods", one of those chivalrous highwaymen who rob the rich to help the poor. They say that once he met a Taoist recluse in the mountains somewhere and wanted to become his disciple. When the old fellow refused, Master Gourd sat down cross-legged under a tree in front of his hermitage for many days so that his legs withered away. Then the old hermit initiated him into all the secrets of life and death.' He paused, pensively rubbing his chin. 'Yes, the four fellows that attacked you must have been Lang's henchmen from the south. Local men would never attack Master Gourd. In the first place because they have a great respect for his wisdom, and second because they believe he possesses magic powers, and can draw out someone's soul and bottle it up in his calabash. But how could they have known that you were going to take that walk, sir?'

'Before answering that, Siew, I want to ask you a straight question. When we were talking here this afternoon, I clearly perceived that besides your concern over Lang and other unwelcome visitors, there were more important issues in the back of your

51

mind. Since, through you, I am getting deeply involved in a situation I know next to nothing about, I demand a full explanation, here and now.'

The captain jumped up and began to pace the floor, sputtering nervously:

'Very sorry, sir! You're absolutely right, of course. Should've told you the whole story, at once. Bad mistake, keeping things back. I . . .'

'Out with it, man! It's getting late, and I am tired!'

'Yes, sir. Well, Colonel Kang is a personal friend of mine, you see. My best friend, in fact. We are natives of the same town, always remained in close touch. It was the colonel who got me transferred here from the capital, wanted a fellow near him he could trust. He's a splendid fellow, old military family. Fine warriors, but no money, of course. And no connections at court. Added to that he's a bit stand-offish, and keeps himself to himself, so you can imagine that when he was made commander in the Water Palace here the people there didn't like it very much. They prefer the toadying kind, the give-and-take fellows, you know. So he has had all kinds of difficulties, but he has always got over them all right. Lately, however, he has been very downcast. I urged him to tell me what was worrying him, but the stubborn fellow would only say it was about something in the palace. Then, on top of that, he had to conduct some investigation or other yesterday —a hell of a ticklish job, he told me; he didn't know how to go about it. Wasn't allowed to tell me a thing, he said, but it was neck or nothing! You can imagine . . .'

'All very interesting, but come to the point!'

'Certainly, sir. Well, when I recognized you, sir, I thought your arrival was a godsend. You know my admiration for you, sir . . . I thought that besides helping me to get a grip on all the high-class crooks here, if I could arrange a meeting between you and my colonel, he might be willing to tell you more about this investigation, and that you, with your magnificent record, sir, might . . .'

Judge Dee raised his hand.

'When exactly did you tell the colonel I was here?'

'When, you say, sir? I met you only this afternoon! I see the colonel only in the mornings, sir, when I go to the palace to hand in my daily report. Meant to tell him about you first thing tomorrow morning!'

'I see.' Judge Dee leaned back in his chair and slowly caressed his sidewhiskers. After a while he said:

'I must ask you, Siew, not to say a word about me to your colonel. I'll be glad to meet him some time, but not just yet. Perhaps you could ask him to arrange a visit to the Water Palace for me, before I leave here. In what part does the famous Third Princess live, by the way?'

'In the north-east corner of the palace grounds, sir. The most secluded and most closely guarded section. In order to get there you have to pass through the residence and the offices of the Chief Eunuch. Capable fellow, I have heard. Has to be, for you know how it is, sir, inside those purple palace walls. Place is riddled with intrigue.'

'I have always heard that the Third Princess is an exceptionally intelligent and capable woman. Couldn't she put an end to all that underhand bickering?'

'She certainly could, provided she knew what was going on! It's the hardest thing for a Princess, sir, to know what is happening among the hundreds of persons in her own palace. She's hedged in on all sides by ladies-in-waiting, court ladies, ladies of the chamber and what have you, and every single one of them twists every bit of news to suit herself. I thank heaven my job is outside those walls, sir!' He shook his head, then asked briskly, 'What do you want me to do about Mr Lang, sir? And what about those four corpses in his godown?'

'As to Lang, nothing at all. I shall deal with him personally, in my own good time. The dead bodies I want removed to your mortuary by a few of your trusted men. They may say they were highway robbers, cut down by a patrol when they attacked a traveller. Oh yes, talking about robbers, I learned some interesting details relating to the murder of the cashier. That young fellow was in love with the innkeeper's wife, and the odds are that she went to Ten Miles Village, the village across the mountains that Tai Min marked on his map. Apparently the idea was that Tai Min would join her there. But he was attacked and killed on the way.'

'That's very interesting,' the captain said slowly. 'Mrs Wei being that kind of woman, she might have another lover too. And jealousy is often a strong motive for murder. Well, it so happens that two of my agents are due to leave for that area this very night. I shall order them to inquire after Mrs Wei. She may be staying in Ten Miles Village together with Tai's murderer, for all we know! Thanks very much, sir!'

As Judge Dee got up, the captain added:

'This attack on you has shocked me, sir. Don't you want two or three of my civilian agents assigned to you, for protection?'

'No, thank you, they would only be in my way. Good-bye, Siew, I'll let you know when I have any news.'

The crestfallen captain conducted him personally downstairs.

Few people were about in the main street, for it was getting on for midnight. Judge Dee fastened the reins of his horse to the pillar by the Kingfisher's entrance and went inside. There was no one about in the hall, but through the lattice screen he could see the back of Mr Wei. The innkeeper stood bent over a large leather box on the floor. The judge walked round the counter and rapped with his knuckles on the screen.

The innkeeper righted himself and turned round. 'What can I do for you, Doctor?' he asked in his dull voice.

'Tell a groom to take my horse to the stables, Mr Wei. After seeing my patient, I went for a ride in the forest and got lost.'

Wei muttered something about keeping late hours and shuffled to the back door of the office. Judge Dee suddenly realized he was dog-tired. He sat down in the armchair beside the desk and stretched his stiff legs. Staring with unseeing eyes at the intricate pattern of the lattice screen, he reviewed the amazing events of that night. He had assumed, as a matter of course, that his summons to the palace had come as a result of information about his arrival supplied by Captain Siew. But the captain had not seen the colonel, and he knew nothing about the theft of the necklace. Someone else in Rivertown must have recognized him, and learned

54

about his alias by consulting the register of the Kingfisher. And that unknown person must have a direct approach to the Princess, for only three hours had elapsed between his arrival in River-town and the Lady Hydrangea sending for him. It was all very puzzling. Somewhere beyond the hall he faintly heard the tinkling sound of a moon-guitar. The player evidently kept late hours.

His eyes strayed to the open box on the floor. It was crammed with articles of women's apparel. More clothes were draped over the backrest of Mr Wei's chair. On top was a long-sleeved jacket of red brocade, with a rather pleasing flower pattern of gold thread.

The innkeeper came back and told him that the groom would take care of his horse.

'Sorry to disturb you so late, Mr Wei.' Judge Dee felt reluctant to get up, so he added casually: 'I noticed a large brick-shed, opposite the stables. That's your storeroom, I suppose?'

The innkeeper darted a quick glance at him, a nasty gleam in his shifty eyes.

'Nothing of value there! Just old sticks of broken furniture, Doctor. I have a hard time trying to make both ends meet, sir! If you knew my expenses. . . .' He took the red jacket and the robe from his chair, threw them into the box and sat down. 'I have been kept so busy these days I haven't even got around to sorting out my dear wife's clothes!' Then he muttered, half to himself, 'Hope the pawnbroker 'll offer a good price! Kept her in luxury, I did!'

'I was distressed to learn about your domestic trouble, Mr Wei. Haven't you got any idea who could have seduced your wife?'

'Wouldn't wonder if he were that tall hoodlum that came to my door sometimes, asking for the post of doorkeeper! Lives in the neighbour district.'

'You could file a charge against him, you know.'

'Against him? No, thank you, sir! The fellow has friends in the mountains. Wouldn't like to wake up with my throat cut! Good riddance to bad rubbish, that's all there is to it, sir.'

Judge Dee rose and wished him a good night.

On the second floor it was dead quiet. Upon entering his room,

55

he found that the servants had put up the shutters at nightfall, so that now it had become hot and stuffy inside. He went to open them, then thought he had better not. No use in inviting assassins to a nightly visit. Having verified that the door could be locked by a solid bolt, he undressed and inspected the wound on his forearm. The cut was long but not deep. After he had cleaned it with hot tea from the tea basket, he put on a new bandage, then stretched himself out on the narrow bed for a good night's rest. But the close air was oppressive; soon he was drenched with sweat. The mutilated face of the bearded man rose before his mind's eye, and he saw the other dead men in horrible detail. Then he reflected that, for a crippled old man, Master Gourd had shown remarkable resolution and skill in fighting. Strange . . . now that he had seen Master Gourd's face clearly in the godown, it seemed vaguely familiar. Could he have met him somewhere before? Mulling this over, he dozed off.

# IX

The judge woke early, after a fitful sleep. He got up and opened the shutters. The clear sky promised a fine sunny day. After he had washed his face and combed his beard, he began to pace the floor, his hands behind his back. Then he suddenly realized he was tarrying only because he hoped Fern would bring the morning tea. Annoyed with himself, he decided he would have breakfast in the Nine Clouds Inn across the street. He had better try to gather some general information about the town, and find out how he could get a good view of the walls of the Water Palace.

Down in the hall the young clerk stood yawning at the counter. Judge Dee muttered a perfunctory reply to his 'Good morning' and crossed the street.

Unlike the Kingfisher, the Nine Clouds had its own restaurant, located behind the main hall. At this early hour only half a dozen customers were scattered around the small tables, gobbling their morning rice. A small rotund man was standing by the counter, berating a surly waiter. He paused to give the judge a sharp look from his little beady eyes, then came waddling to meet him.

'An honour to receive a famous doctor from the capital, sir! Please take this corner table, quiet and cosy! You'll find our food better than anything the Kingfisher can offer you, sir. May I recommend rice fried with pork and onions, and crisp fried trout, fresh from the river?'

Judge Dee wanted a more frugal breakfast, but it might be worth engaging the garrulous innkeeper in some further talk. He nodded, and the fat man shouted the order at the waiter.

'I found the rooms in the Kingfisher quite comfortable,' the judge remarked, 'but I don't want to make any demands on the service, for that terrible murder of the cashier has upset the routine.'

'Yes, sir, Tai Min was a good man at his job, and a quiet, pleasant youngster. But it was Mrs Wei who ran the place, sir. Fine, capable woman, but the way that niggardly husband treated her! Kept an eye on every single copper she spent, you know! When she dropped in here, I always gave her a couple of dumplings stuffed with sweet beans—our speciality, you know. She was mighty fond of those. Gave her three or four the very night she went away, as a matter of fact. I don't hold with married women doing things they shouldn't do, sir, not me. But Wei drove her to it, and that's a fact!' He gave a sign to the waiter and went on, 'And she always thought of the business first. Didn't want to run off before she had shown that niece of hers all the ropes. A looker, that young wench, but a bit uppish, if you ask me. Mrs Wei, she was what you might call a conscientious housewife. Wish I could say the same of my own missus. . . .'

The waiter brought a bamboo tray heaped with dumplings.

'Here you are, Doctor!' the innkeeper said, beaming at him. 'Take as many as you like, on the house!'

Judge Dee took a bite but found them much too sweet for his taste. 'Delicious!' he exclaimed.

'They are all yours, sir!' The fat man leaned over the table and resumed confidentially, 'Now I've something that'll interest you, sir. Poses a problem for you, professionally. Every time I have a meal, after about half an hour or so I get a dull pain here in my left side. Then I get a burning feeling, right here above my navel, and a sour feeling, deep in . . .'

'I charge one silver piece for a consultation,' the judge pointed out gently. 'Payable in advance.'

'One whole silver piece! But you don't need to examine me, you know. Just wanted to have your opinion. I am suffering from constipation too. Now I . . .'

'See your doctor,' the judge said curtly and took up his chopsticks. The fat man gave him a hurt look and waddled back to the counter, taking the tray of dumplings with him.

The judge ate with gusto. He had to admit that the fried trout were indeed very good. When he left the Nine Clouds he saw Fern standing in the portico across the street. She wore a brown jacket and wide trousers, and a red sash round her waist; her hair was bound up with a red cloth. She wished the judge a cheerful 'Good morning', and added:

'Weather is fine! What about our trip up river?'

'Shouldn't I change?'

'Oh no. We'll just have to buy straw hats on the way.'

She took him down several narrow alleys that brought them in a few minutes to the east end of the quay. He bought two straw hats. While she was busy tying the ribbon of hers under her chin, he cast a quick glance at the godowns. Two coolies were carrying a bale to the clearing, supervised by a thin man with a large, bullet-shaped head. Fern went down the stone steps leading to the water, and pointed at a narrow, sleek boat moored among the larger rivercraft. While she held it steady, Judge Dee stepped inside and sat down in the stern. Skilfully she poled the boat out from among the other craft, then exchanged the pole for a long oar. As she started sculling the boat into midstream, the judge said:

'You know, I wouldn't mind having a look at the famous Water Palace.'

'That's easy enough! We'll go along this bank and pass it before crossing over. The best places are all over the other side, you see.'

There was a slight breeze over the placid brown water, but the morning sun was hot on Judge Dee's face. He stuffed his cap into his sleeve, and put the round straw hat on his head. Fern had taken off her jacket. A red scarf was wound tightly round her well-formed bosom. Leaning back in the bow, the judge looked at her standing there in the stern, moving the long sculling oar with graceful ease. Her shoulders and arms had a golden tan. He reflected—a little sadly—that there was no substitute for youth. Then he turned his attention to the riverbank. Tall pine trees grew close to the water's edge, rising up from the tangled undergrowth. Here and there he noticed the narrow mouths of inlets and coves.

'You won't catch anything worth while in there,' she remarked. 'Just a few crabs and mud-fish. It's too early in the year for eels.'

As they moved upstream, the forest thickened. Moss-covered liana clung to the low branches overhanging the water. After about a quarter of an hour Fern turned the boat into mid-stream.

'Can't we follow the bank a little further?' the judge said quickly. 'We must be getting near to the palace and I'd like to have a good look at it.'

'And get both of us killed? Don't you see those painted buoys ahead? Over on that quay there's a notice in letters as large as your head ordering all craft to stay outside those buoys. And on the bank beyond the palace there is the same polite notice. If you cross the line, the archers on the battlements will use you for target practice with their crossbows. You'll have to admire the palace from a good distance!'

She sculled the boat in a broad curve round the buoys. Then he saw the three-storeyed watch-tower, at the north-west corner of the palace compound. The wood ended abruptly at a narrow inlet, evidently the mouth of the moat surrounding the palace. The north wall rose directly from the water at a slightly receding angle. The crenellated ramparts were interrupted at regular intervals by lower watch-towers. The sun glittered on the spiked helmets of the archers manning the battlements.

'Quite a pile, eh?' Fern called over to him from the stern.

'Rather. Let's go a little farther till we are opposite the north-east tower. Then I'll have seen everything!'

A large cargo junk glided past, the rowers swinging the long oars to the rhythm of a plaintive song. Fern joined them in her clear young voice, adjusting her sculling to the quicker beat. The judge thought the wall looked very high and forbidding. He counted eight barred archways, just above the water, evidently the gates that fed the canals and watercourses inside. Then he saw the pavilion, jutting out from the wall just above the last water-gate. It was a kind of covered balcony of trapezoid shape, with three bay windows, a large one in front flanked by two smaller ones. He estimated that the bottom of the buttress supporting the pavilion was about six feet above the water. A small boat moored there would be invisible from above. But how could a boat get in there without being spotted by the archers on the watch-towers?

'You hoping to see the beautiful princess at the window? What about crossing over to the other bank now?'

Judge Dee nodded. It had been heavy going upstream; Fern's shoulders glistened moistly in the sun that was steadily gaining in strength. The north bank was less thickly wooded; here and there a fisherman's thatched hut appeared among the green foliage. When they were close Fern threw a hook weighted with two bricks into the water. The boat floated down the stream for a while, then the anchor caught and it lay still. She said with satisfaction:

'This is just about the right place. When I was here with Tai Min the other day, we caught a couple of fine perches. Look, in this jar are the crabs' legs, the very best bait!'

'Our Master Confucius always fished with a rod,' the judge remarked as he prepared the bait, 'never with a net. He thought the fish ought to be given a sporting chance.'

'I know the quotation. When father was still alive he used to read the Classics with me. He was the head of our village school, you see. Since mother died when I was still young, and I was the only child, father spent a lot of his time on me. No, take that other line! You need a longer one for perch.' Throwing out her own line, she added, 'We had a very happy life. But when father died I had to move to the inn here, for Uncle Wei was the nearest relative. I couldn't take along the books we used to read; they belonged to the school. You being a learned doctor, you must have got a large library, haven't you?'

'Fairly large. But little time to use it.'

'I'd like to live in a scholar's home, you know. Read books about all kinds of interesting subjects, practise painting and calligraphy. Makes you feel secure, if you know what I mean. When my aunt was still there it wasn't so bad in the Kingfisher, mind you. Uncle never gave her much for her clothes, but she inherited a few bolts of good silk, and I helped her make new robes from them. Her favourite jacket was made of red brocade, with flowers

61

in gold thread. She thought it suited her very well, and she was right too!'

The judge lowered his line into the brown water. Settling back in the bow, he said:

'Yes, I heard that your aunt was a nice woman. I can well understand an impressionable youngster like Tai Min conceiving a kind of calf-love for her.'

'He was absolutely crazy about her! I am sure he began to gamble just because he wanted to be able to give her a present now and then!'

'Gambling is a sure way to lose money instead of making it,' the judge said absent-mindedly. He thought he felt a slight tug at the line.

'Tai Min won. But I think that Mr Lang let him win on purpose, the better to fleece him afterwards! That Lang gives me the creeps!'

'Lang? Where did they gamble?'

'Oh, Tai Min went to Lang's wing a few times. Hey, watch it!'

He let the line slip through his fingers. In a flash he saw a pattern emerging. Lang would never have befriended the young cashier without a good reason.

'Give him more line!' Fern called out excitedly.

Yes, he would give Lang rope. Lots of rope. It might lead to the link connecting Lang's ramshackle godown with the golden palace gates. Alternately slackening and tightening the line, he tried to survey the consequences of his discovery.

'Pull him in!' she hissed.

Slowly gathering in the line, he saw a fair-sized perch come to the surface. He leaned over the gunwale and got the squirming fish on board and into the basket.

'Well done! Now watch me!' She stared at her floater, her face flushed. The breeze shifted a stray strand of glossy hair from under her straw hat. The judge was eager to get back to the south bank, for he wanted to go ashore and check whether there was perhaps a pathway there. But it would be cruel to spoil her pleasure. He threw out a short line and again went over in his mind the various possibilities. The fact that the cashier had been

THE JUDGE CATCHES A PERCH

tortured had struck him at once as curious. Now he saw a possible explanation. Her voice roused him.

'They won't bite at all. Tell me, how many wives do you have?'

'Three.'

'Is your First a nice lady?'

'Very. I have a happy and harmonious household, I am glad to say.'

'You being a famous doctor, you should have four. Even numbers bring good luck! And speaking about luck, I think . . .'

She tugged at her line, and brought up a smaller fish. Then they remained silent for a long time, she intent on her line, he occupied with his own thoughts. After she had caught a fairly large perch, the judge remarked:

'My legs are getting a bit cramped. I'd like to try my hand at sculling the boat. Haven't done it for many a year!'

'All right! As long as you don't overturn the boat!'

Crouching on the bottom, they exchanged places. The boat began to rock, and he had to steady her with his arm round her shoulders. 'It's very nice to be with you!' she whispered.

Judge Dee quickly took the long oar. He knelt in the stern and moved the boat upstream a little so that she could haul the anchor up. Then he turned the boat away from shore. It didn't go too badly, but in his kneeling position he could not use his body weight and had to depend on his arms alone. The wound on his forearm began to throb. He tried to get to his feet, but the boat began to rock dangerously. She burst out in peals of laughter.

'Well, I'll manage without standing,' he said sourly.

'Where are you heading for?'

'I'd like to go ashore somewhere. I might find some medicinal herbs in the undergrowth over there. Do you mind?'

'I don't. But you won't be able to do more than poke about a little around the small coves. There is no path of any sort.'

'In that case we'll head back for the quay. It'll be easy; we'll have the current with us.'

He soon found, however, that it was easier said than done. There was much traffic now, and it took all his skill to avoid collisions. He listened to her with half an ear as she chattered away happily. Suddenly he asked:

'Searched? Who searched what?'

'My uncle, I said! He must have searched poor Tai Min's attic. When I tidied it up this morning, I noticed someone had been over it with a fine comb! Can't imagine what uncle expected to find there! I'll take over here; you'll never manage to berth it properly!'

# X

They parted on the landing-stage. Fern took the main street, carrying the fish-basket and humming a song. Judge Dee walked past the fish-market and entered the first small eating-place he saw. He ordered a large bowl of noodles stewed with bamboo sprouts. After a quick cup of tea he went back to the Kingfisher, for he was eager to take a bath.

As he had expected, the bath was empty, for it was the hour of the noon rice; even the bath-attendant was off duty. Stretched out in the pool, he carefully considered the move he was contemplating. It was a long shot, a very long shot. His theory was based on only two facts: first, that the poor cashier Tai Min had been severely tortured prior to his being killed; and second, that his room had been searched. All the rest was mere guess-work, based on his knowledge of the mean, grasping nature of men like Lang Liu. Yes, he would risk it. If his theory should prove correct, he would have successfully completed the first phase of his investigation. If he was wrong, he would at least have frightened a few people. And frightened people are liable to make bad mistakes.

The bath-attendant came in while Judge Dee was putting a new bandage on his forearm. He told him to fetch clean robes from his room and to give the soiled ones to the laundrywomen. Clad in his brown travelling-robe, now crisply laundered, he went to the hall and asked the clerk if Mr Lang had finished his noon rice. When the clerk nodded he gave him his visiting-card and told him to inquire whether Mr Lang could see him for a few moments.

'Mr Lang doesn't like to be disturbed directly after his meals, Doctor!'

'Ask him anyway!'

The clerk went down the corridor with a doubtful look, but he came back with a broad smile. 'Mr Lang says you're welcome, sir ! It's the fourth door on your right.'

Judge Dee was admitted by a thin man with a bullet-shaped head, the one he had seen that morning by the godowns. He introduced himself with an obsequious smile as Mr Lang's accountant, then took the judge through a large, cool ante-room to a vast chamber that seemed to take up the entire rear of the inn's left wing. Evidently this was the most secluded and most expensive suite of the Kingfisher.

Mr Lang was sitting behind a heavy desk of carved ebony, a bulky ledger in front of him. The two bodyguards stood by the folding doors that gave onto the neglected back garden. Mr Lang rose and with a courteous bow invited the judge to take the other armchair. He said with a thin smile:

'I was just going over this ledger with my accountant. Your esteemed visit provides me with a most welcome interruption of that tedious task !' He motioned the accountant to serve tea.

'I had planned to pay you a courtesy call earlier, Mr Lang,' Judge Dee began affably, 'but I had a late night, and this morning I felt a bit out of sorts. The weather is fine today, sir.' He accepted the cup the accountant offered him and took a sip.

'Apart from the rainy days,' Mr Lang remarked, 'I find the climate here quite agreeable.'

The judge set his teacup down hard. Putting his hands on his knees, he said, harshly now:

'Glad to hear that, Lang ! For you'll have to stay here in Rivertown for a long, long time.'

His host gave him a sharp look. He asked slowly:

'What exactly do you mean by that?'

'I mean that the truce is off. We'll get you as soon as you put one foot out of this special area, Lang. Last night your stupid henchmen took me to your godown on the quay and tried to kill me.'

'I told you there was blood all over the floor, boss. I . . .' the accountant muttered.

'Shut up !' Lang told him. And to the two bodyguards: 'Close those damned doors ! One of you stand outside in the garden, the other in the ante-room. Let no one disturb us.' Then he fixed the judge with his large eyes that now had a hard glint. 'I don't know what you are talking about. I suspected you were a Red when I saw you in the bath yesterday morning. Doctors don't come with a boxer's build, generally. But I deny having tried to get you killed. Our side is keeping to the truce.'

Judge Dee shrugged.

'I'll let that go, for the moment. There's a much more important matter to discuss. My orders are to make you a proposal. You employed the cashier of this inn to steal a very nice bauble. Your league must be getting short on cash, Lang—seeing that you are risking being cut to pieces. Slowly and expertly.'

Lang retained his impassive mien, but the judge noticed that the accountant's face was filled with a sickly pallor. He resumed:

'It would be a pleasure to denounce you to the authorities, Lang. But a truce is a truce, and my people stick to their word. Provided, of course, that we share. Half of eighty-four makes forty-two. Please correct me if my figures are wrong, will you?'

Lang slowly tugged at his goatee, fixing his two bodyguards with a baleful look. The two big men made frantic gestures of denial. The accountant hastily retreated behind his master's chair. For a long while it was very silent in the large room. At last Lang said:

'Your people are good, very good. I'll have to overhaul my own organization. Thoroughly. Yes, your figures are correct—it was agreed that on neutral territory we should share and share alike. I didn't let your boss know, however, because the whole thing fell through. I haven't got the pearls.'

Judge Dee rose abruptly.

'Last night's attempt to kill me proves you are lying, Lang. My orders are that, should you refuse our reasonable request, I am to inform you that the truce is ended. Which I do here and now. Good-bye!'

He went to the door. When he had put his hand on the knob Lang suddenly called out: 'Come back and sit down! I'll explain the situation.'

The judge came back to the desk but he didn't take the chair offered. He said in a surly voice:

'First of all I want you to apologize for trying to have me murdered, Lang!'

'I apologize for the fact that you were inconvenienced in a go-down that belongs to me, and I shall have the matter looked into at once. That satisfactory?'

'It's better than nothing.' Judge Dee sat down again. Lang leaned back in his chair.

'I made a mistake, shouldn't have accepted the job. But you know our expenses nowadays! I have to pay the directors of my gambling establishments a fortune in salaries, and yet the scoundrels are cheating on the proceeds. And how can you run decent brothels when even farm-girls are in short supply? We have to pay as much for a peasant girl as for a trained courtesan! Unless we get some real good floods or a long drought and crop failure, I am going to lose on that branch. As to taxes, let me tell you that . . .'

'Don't!' Judge Dee interrupted. 'Tell me about pearls!'

'Well, I just wanted to explain to you that, things being what they are at present, ten gold bars is a round sum not to be sneezed at. And there were ten gold bars for me in that affair, and practically no risk or expense.' Lang heaved a deep sigh. 'This is what happened. Last week a silk broker comes to see me—Hao he calls himself. Brings a letter of introduction from one of my men in the capital. Hao says he has a contact who has formulated a plan to steal a valuable necklace from the Water Palace here. The thing has eighty-four pearls of the best quality, he says, but they'll have to be sold one by one, of course. If I know of someone who's familiar with the river and the area around the palace, and get him to do the job, Hao's contact 'll pay me ten gold bars. I think at once of the cashier here, who knows every inch of the river, but I say nothing doing. Ten gold bars is a lot of money, but stealing from the palace is too much of a risk. Then, however, Hao explains all the arrangements made. My accountant 'll repeat them—he has a phenomenal memory. (It's the only good point he's got, the fathead!) Speak up, you! Say your lesson!'

The bullet-headed man closed his eyes. Clasping his hands, he rattled off:

'The man is to leave town by boat one hour before midnight, row to the fourth cove on the right bank, leave the boat there and take the path behind the second row of pine trees. Formerly used by the palace patrols, it leads all along the river bank to the north-west corner of the palace moat. About two feet under the surface there's an old sluice door; swim along it to the corner of the north-west watch-tower. Just above water level a ledge about a foot wide runs all along the north wall. Walk along it till you arrive at the last water-gate. Above it is a buttress that supports a covered balcony. There are many cracks among the bricks; the wall can easily be scaled. Enter the pavilion by the side-window. The pavilion is connected with a bedroom by an open, moon-shaped doorway. The necklace 'll be lying either on the dressing-table just inside that moon-door, or on the tea-table opposite. Remain outside the moon-door and make sure the people are asleep. Then step inside, take the necklace, and go back the same way. No need to worry about the archers on the ramparts—they'll be busy elsewhere.'

The thin man opened his eyes and smiled smugly. Lang resumed:

'Since Hao's contact was evidently a man who knew what he was talking about, I thought I might as well see whether I could rope in the cashier. I knew he needed money. I invited him for a friendly gambling-bout, let him win at first, then lose heavily. When I told him about the planned theft, as a favour, he agreed at once. So I told Hao it was all right. If Tai Min was caught, I would, of course, disclaim all knowledge of the scheme, and point out that the boy had been tempted because he had lost all his money at the gambling-table.'

'I'll take your word for all that, Lang,' the judge said wearily. 'I am still waiting to hear why you didn't get the necklace. The rest we'll take for granted!'

'I just want to give you the whole picture,' Lang said, annoyed. 'Well, Tai Min started from my godown at the time indicated. He promised to come straight back there, deliver up the necklace, and get his twenty silver pieces, minus what he owed me. Now I admit I make mistakes sometimes, but at least I know the routine work. I posted a couple of my men on the roads leading west, east and south from this town—just to make sure that if Tai inadvertently forgot about our appointment in the godown, we would be able to remind him, you see. My accountant waited for Tai in the godown for a couple of hours, in vain. Then the fellow was brought in by the two men who'd been watching the road east. They had caught Tai Min galloping blithely along, and nicely dressed too. He had gone back to the Kingfisher first, you see.'

The judge suppressed a yawn.

'You must spend a lot of your time listening to the story-tellers in the market, Lang!' Then, harshly: 'What about the necklace?'

'The bastard said he never got it! Everything went all right to the point where he had scaled the wall and was inside the pavilion. There was no one about, there, or in the bedroom. And no necklace, no baubles at all worth the taking. He came back, but didn't dare to keep our appointment. He said he was afraid we'd think he was deceiving us and had hidden the necklace somewhere. Well, by an odd coincidence, that was exactly what my men thought he had done. They tried hard to make him tell the truth—so hard that he died on their hands. I don't know how well your league is managing with personnel, but as for me, I don't seem to be able to get any really good men any more.' He sadly shook his head and went on: 'Not only did they bungle the questioning of that thieving cashier, they also chose the wrong place to heave his body into the river. It ought to have been found a couple of miles downstream. As a matter of routine, I had Tai Min's attic here in the inn searched. Found nothing, of course. And I can't search every hollow tree and every nook and cranny of that blasted pine forest, can I? So I've written off the necklace, and that's all there is to it.'

Judge Dee heaved a deep sigh.

'It's a nice story, Lang. Just as nice as the one Tai Min told to your men. The only difference is that he couldn't prove his story, while you can. Just by introducing me to your good friend, Mr Hao.'

71

Lang shifted uneasily in his chair.

'Hao was supposed to turn up here yesterday morning. With the ten gold bars. But he didn't. And I don't know where to find him.'

There was a long silence. Then Judge Dee pushed his chair back and got up.

'I am very sorry, Lang, but I can't go back home with that story. I'm not calling you a liar, mind you; I'm just saying I must have proof. I'll be staying on here for a bit, in order to observe the situation, so to speak. Needless to say, I have a few friends hanging about here too, so don't repeat your mistake of last night! Should you feel like having another friendly chat, you know where my room is. Good-bye!'

The bullet-headed accountant conducted him respectfully to the door.

# XI

Up in his room Judge Dee sat down heavily in the armchair by the window. The murder of Tai Min had been solved now. He would see to it that Lang Liu and the men who tortured and killed the unfortunate cashier would get their deserts. But first he would have to identify the real criminals who had planned the theft of the necklace. For now his surmise had been proved right: the theft was the essential part of some complicated court intrigue, and the contact of the mysterious Mr Hao must be inside the palace. It was only to be expected that there would be a Mr Hao, for when depraved courtiers want to hire professionals from outside to do their dirty work, they always employ a 'broker'. If only he could lay hands on Mr Hao! Arrested and interrogated, Hao would tell who his contact was. But something had gone wrong somewhere: Hao had not contacted Lang, and the judge had the uneasy feeling that Mr Hao had disappeared from the scene for good.

Again the soft sound of the moon-guitar came from the room below. A quick melody this time, expertly played; unfamiliar but quite attractive. It ended on an abrupt chord, then a woman laughed. There were no courtesans in Rivertown, but apparently some guests had brought their own girl friends along. Judge Dee tugged pensively at his moustache.

What could Tai Min have done with the necklace? It had been easy enough to grab it from the side-table where the Princess had put it. The cashier could have reached it even without stepping inside the pavilion. Could one of the plotters have been waiting for Tai Min, behind the bars of the water-gate, underneath the buttress? The water-gates had low arches, no higher than three or four feet, as the judge had seen for himself from the river, but presumably the underground canal could be negotiated in a small, flat-bottomed boat. The man could then have taken the necklace and handed Tai Min a reward through the iron grating; perhaps one gold bar, instead of the ten promised to Lang. The plotters in the palace were experts in intrigue, and it would not be beyond them to play such a trick on Lang. And the same transaction could have taken place in the pine forest—Mr Hao waiting there for Tai Min to return. In either case Tai Min could have hidden the gold bar, in a hollow tree, possibly, planning to retrieve it at a later date, after he and Mrs Wei had discussed their future in Ten Miles Village. The judge heaved a deep sigh. There were too many possibilities, too many unknown factors.

One thing was certain: Lang Liu had had nothing to do with the murderous attack on himself and Master Gourd. The killers had taken them to Lang's godown only because they knew Lang used the place for torturing victims and other dirty work, and that it was convenient, the neighbourhood being deserted at night. They had been hired by the same 'Mr Hao' for that was the name the bearded leader had just managed to pronounce before he died. The plotters' first attempt on his own life had failed. But they were apparently determined that he should not interfere with their scheme, and therefore he would have to reckon with a second attack. He sat up. There was a slight tap at his door.

Judge Dee took his sword from the side-table, pushed the bolt back and opened the door a few inches, his sword ready. It was Lang's accountant.

'Mr Lang asks you to step into the hall, sir. He has just received a message he wants to show you.'

The judge put his sword back on the table and followed the bullet-headed man down the broad staircase. Mr Lang stood at the counter, talking to the innkeeper.

'Ah, Doctor, glad you are still at home! One of my clerks has a bad stomach attack. I would be very grateful if you would have a look at him. I'll show you his room!' About to turn round, Lang groped in his sleeve and brought out an open envelope, addressed to him in large, well-written characters. He showed it to Wei and asked: 'By the way, who delivered this letter just now, Mr Wei?'

'I was at my desk behind the lattice screen, sir. I only got a glimpse of the street urchin. He threw it on the counter and

74

THE INNKEEPER TELLS MR LANG ABOUT A LETTER

rushed off. When I saw it was addressed to you, I had the clerk take it to your suite at once.'

'I see. Well, come along, Doctor.'

When the three men were back in Lang's study, the gangster handed the envelope to Judge Dee.

'You wanted proof,' he said dryly. 'The little scene at the counter I staged for your benefit, to show you the letter was actually delivered here, and not a forgery made by me after you had left us just now.'

The judge unfolded the single sheet. It said that the undersigned regretted that unavoidable circumstances had prevented him from visiting Lang on the appointed day, to discuss the purchase of the raw silk. Today, however, he would be in Lang's godown at six. If the samples of silk were satisfactory, the deal would be concluded then and there. It was signed 'Hao'. The style was impeccable, the writing, the formal, regular hand used in chanceries. It was doubtless genuine, for it would have taken Lang at least a day to find in Rivertown a scholar who could write such a letter. Handing it back to Lang, the judge said:

'All right. This is indeed the proof I wanted, Lang. Our truce continues, as agreed. I shall be at the godown at six.'

Mr Lang raised his thin eyebrows.

'At the godown? You don't think we are going there, do you? The whole thing is off! Hao'll find no one there, and the door locked!'

Judge Dee gave him a pitying look.

'No wonder you can't get good personnel, Lang. You are losing your power of judgement! Heavens, man, here are ten solid gold bars coming to you, and you lock your door and put up a notice that you aren't at home! Listen to me, my friend, I'll tell you exactly what we'll do! We shall receive Mr Hao very politely, and inquire whether he has the gold with him. If so, we'll gratefully accept it. Adding that we didn't get the necklace, but that we went to a hell of a lot of trouble and expense on his behalf, and that we are willing to consider the ten bars as an amicable settlement.'

Lang shook his head.

'That dogshead Hao must represent powerful people. High

76

officials by the smell of it. Or friends of palace officials, seeing they knew so much about the lay-out of the place. I am a man of peace, brother, I don't like trouble.'

'Don't you see that we have them in the hollow of our hand, Lang, high officials or not? If Mr Hao doesn't like our fair proposal, we say that as law-abiding citizens we are perfectly willing to go together with him to the Headquarters of the Guard, and let the authorities decide the case. We shall then have to explain, of course, that we went along with the criminal proposal to steal an Imperial treasure only because we wanted to have full proof of the outrage before reporting it. And now we claim the government reward.'

Lang hit his fist on the table.

'By heaven!' he shouted. 'Now I understand why your league always gets the best of us. You have real men, while I must make do with stupid sons of dogs like this self-styled accountant!' He jumped up and viciously slapped the bullet-headed man twice. Having thus given vent to his feelings, he resumed his seat and told the judge with a broad smile: 'It's a beautiful, a splendid plan, colleague!'

'It means five gold bars to us,' Judge Dee remarked dryly. 'Four for the league, and one for me, as commission.'

'Your leaders ought to give you two!' Lang said generously. He snapped at the accountant, 'This is your last chance to make good, fathead! You go to the godown with our colleague here.' And to the judge: 'I can't afford to go personally, of course. I have my reputation to consider. But you two won't be alone, for I shall post a dozen or so good men in the godown behind mine.' He shot the judge a quick look and added hurriedly, 'Just in case our Mr Hao brings a couple of men with him, you see!'

'Yes, I quite see your point!' the judge said coldly. 'I'll be in the godown a little before six. Tell your men to let me pass, will you?' He went to the door, and Mr Lang saw him personally to the corridor, saying jovially:

'It was a pleasure making your acquaintance, colleague! We'll have a drink here together afterwards. To the friendly co-operation of the Blues and the Reds!'

77

## XII

Judge Dee went to his room to fetch his calabash and his sword. He had to see Captain Siew at once, tell him about the meeting in the godown, and make arrangements with him for the arrest of the mysterious Mr Hao and Lang's hoodlums.

Fern was standing at the front entrance of the Kingfisher, haggling with an old woman selling toilet articles. He was about to pass her with a friendly nod, when she laid her hand on his arm and showed him an ivory comb, set with cheap jewels. 'Do you think this one would suit me?' she asked coyly. When he bent over to look at it she quickly told him in a whisper: 'Watch out! The two men outside were asking after you.'

'It'll suit you very well,' he said and stepped out on the portico. Feigning to inspect the sky, he saw out of the corner of his eye two gentlemen standing at the gate of the Nine Clouds. Their sedate costume, grey robes with black sashes and black caps, gave them a nondescript character. They might belong to Lang's league, or they might be agents from the palace. And from now on he would have to reckon also with agents of the Red League, who might have learned that he was masquerading as one of their own. Whoever they were, they must not know that he was going to visit Captain Siew.

He strolled up the main street, occasionally halting to inspect the wares displayed in the shop fronts. Yes, the two men in grey were following him. In vain he tried a few well-known dodges. He would round a corner at a leisurely pace, then suddenly rush ahead and try to get lost in the crowd, but the two men stayed behind him, and without any apparent effort. They were old hands at the game. Getting annoyed, the judge went into a large eating-house and chose a table at the back. When the waiter came to take his order he told him he had forgotten something and ran outside by the kitchen door. But one of the gentlemen in grey was standing at the corner of the back alley. The judge walked back to the main street. If he had known the town well, he might have had another try at eluding his pursuers. As it was, he had to resort to a trick that would force them to show what they were, and at the same time get him to Headquarters.

He went along with the stream of traffic till he spotted the spiked helmets of guardsmen ahead. Then he suddenly quickened his pace, halted abruptly and turned round. As he bumped into the taller of the two pursuers, he shouted at the top of his voice: 'Pickpockets! Hold them!'

At once a small crowd gathered round them, asking excited questions. 'I am a doctor!' Judge Dee shouted. 'This tall scoundrel bumped into me while the other tried to put his hand into my sleeve!'

A burly coolie grabbed the tall man by his collar. 'Shame! To rob a doctor! I'll . . .'

'What's all this?' A squat sergeant had pushed his way towards them. The two men in grey had made no move to flee. The elder one told the sergeant quietly:

'This man is falsely accusing us. Take us to your captain!'

The sergeant quickly looked the judge and his two opponents over. Hitching up his swordbelt, he told the coolie:

'Let the gentleman go! It's all a misunderstanding, if you ask me. But my captain 'll decide. Come along, gentlemen, the office is right ahead.'

While they were walking to Headquarters the two men in grey maintained a haughty silence. Lieutenant Liu took them up to the captain's office.

Captain Siew looked up from his papers. Ignoring Judge Dee, he curtly ordered the sergeant to report, then he held out his hand. 'Your papers, please!'

The two men in grey put similar papers on the desk; each had red edges and bore a number of stamps. The elder told the captain:

'This so-called doctor is an imposter. We have orders to take him to the palace. We want a military escort at once.'

Captain Siew pushed his helmet back.

79

'You know I can't do that, gentlemen! Not without a warrant issued by my commander. Doctor Liang's document is quite in order. Properly registered here by my own office, I see.' He scratched his nose. 'Tell you what I'll do, though. You take a note from me to Colonel Kang, then you come back here for this gentleman.' He selected a blank from the papers before him and moistened his writing-brush.

'Come back here to find our man gone?' the elder man asked with a sneer. 'We have explicit orders, Captain!'

'Sorry, but I have my orders too, sir!' Siew rapidly filled out the form, and pushed it across the desk. 'Here you are!'

While the other put it in his sleeve, he said curtly:

'You'll keep this man under detention pending our return.'

'Only if the doctor is agreeable, sir. Can't detain a properly registered citizen without a warrant. "Benevolent rule", you know! On the other hand, if the doctor is willing to co-operate . . .'

'Of course!' the judge said quickly. 'I don't want the rascal these gentlemen are mistaking me for to get away. The misunderstanding must be set right as quickly as possible.'

'Well, then all is settled!' the captain said beaming on them. 'You want horses, gentlemen?'

'We have our own.' The two men in grey turned round without another word. The sergeant took them downstairs.

'D'you know those two stick-in-the-muds?' the captain asked Liu.

'Yes, sir. They belong to the Superintendent's Office. They wear grey; the agents of the Chief Eunuch wear black.'

The captain cast a worried look at Judge Dee.

'You said it, sir! You're certainly getting involved!'

'How long will it take them to come back here?'

'An hour and a half, sir. Two hours, perhaps, if they don't find my colonel in his office.'

'That won't do. I must be in Lang's godown at six. I'm meeting Lang's accountant, and a man who calls himself Hao, a dangerous criminal. Lang doesn't trust Hao or me, and he is putting a dozen or so of his men in the godown opposite his own. I want you to throw a cordon round the godowns, arrest the whole lot of them. Can you spare sixty guardsmen tonight?'

'Depends on what you are going to charge all these people with, sir.'

'Lang's men with the murder of the cashier Tai Min. The others with a crime against the State.'

The captain gave him a searching look.

'In that case I'd better be there myself, sir. Now about those panjandrums from the palace. I am not so sure my colonel 'll issue the warrant. I said in my note that you are duly registered, and he'll want more particulars first.'

'I have reason to assume,' the judge said quietly, 'that the Superintendent will give Colonel Kang a great many particulars.'

Captain Siew turned to the lieutenant.

'What about staging a nice break from prison, eh, Liu?' When the lieutenant nodded with a pleased grin, Siew continued to Judge Dee, 'Liu'll also disguise you properly, sir, so that you can leave here now unnoticed. Wouldn't wonder if those fellows had left a few colleagues to watch this building. Liu is a master in make-up!' Rubbing his hands, he gave the judge a judicious look. 'We start by trimming your beard and whiskers. Then . . .'

'I don't want any mummery!' the judge told him coldly. 'Can your lieutenant get me an old donkey and a pair of crutches?'

Liu nodded and went out at once.

'Wonderful fellow, Liu!' the captain said. 'Have a cup of tea, sir!' Then he gave the judge a circumstantial account of how Liu would make it appear that there was a prisoner in one of the cells downstairs, and how he would fake a break from that cell. He went into every detail with boyish delight. When he had finished he asked, 'What about the murder of that cashier Tai Min, sir?'

'That crime falls under your jurisdiction, Siew, for it was committed right here.' He told him that Lang had admitted having had Tai Min tortured and killed because the cashier had refused to tell Lang where he had hidden the necklace he had been hired to steal. 'When you have arrested Lang's men tonight, we shall go to the Kingfisher and arrest Lang himself, and then I shall formally charge him with the crime. But that man Hao I mentioned is far more important than Lang. As soon as Hao has arrived in the godown, I shall whistle twice on my fingers; then you let your men swoop down on them. Hao may have people with him, though. Let me give you a rough idea of the ground.'

He took a piece of paper and made a sketch of the clearing and the godowns. The captain compared it with his own map, and pointed out where he would post his men. Then Lieutenant Liu came back.

'Donkey is ready in the backyard, sir,' he announced. 'You'd better go quickly, for there's nobody watching outside. Not yet.'

Judge Dee hurriedly thanked the captain. Liu took him down a flight of rickety stairs to a small kitchen yard. While the judge was mounting the ancient donkey, Liu handed him a pair of well-worn crutches.

'Good work!' he whispered to the lieutenant and rode through the narrow gate.

Letting his shoulders sag and keeping his head down, he guided his donkey to the street running parallel to the main thoroughfare. He was banking on Master Gourd being such a familiar figure in Rivertown, that people would take him for granted and not look at him too closely. The only obvious difference was that he carried a sword. He quickly unstrapped it, and wedged it in between the crutches across the donkey's rump.

The donkey walked along sedately, picking its way through the milling crowd. Judge Dee noted with satisfaction that no one gave him a second look. Now and then someone called out a greeting, to which he replied by raising his hand. He drove his mount in the direction of the Kingfisher, for he didn't want to tempt providence too long, and his inn would be the last place where the agents from the palace would expect him to hide.

The narrow alley at the back of the Kingfisher was completely deserted. The bustle of the noon meal was just over, the servants were taking a rest and the tradesmen would not be coming till an hour or so before the evening rice. The judge dismounted at the back door and peered inside at the untidy garden. The folding doors of Lang's suite were closed and no sounds came from the kitchen. The window of his own room on the second floor was shuttered, but the one of the room below was half-open. Someone was strumming a moon-guitar, the same melody the judge had heard on his first night there. Now he remembered it. The tune had been popular in the capital many years ago. Having observed the garden for a while, he decided that the old storehouse would serve his purpose. The door stood ajar, and he slipped inside, the crutches and his sword under his arm.

The shed did not look very inviting. Cobwebs were hanging down from the mouldy rafters, and there was a musty, unpleasant smell. Broken chairs and tables were stacked up against the back wall, but the floor was swept clean. When he had a closer look at the old furniture he discovered behind it a heap of hemp sacks, piled up against the wall.

He shoved a rickety table out of the way and prodded the sacks with the point of his sword. They contained paddy-husks. He decided they would do as a bed for a few hours. The donkey would doubtless amble back to wherever it had come from. After he had stood the crutches against the wall beside the single, barred window, he rearranged the sacks, then laid himself down on top, close to the wall. With his hands cupped behind his head, he reviewed the latest developments.

Mr Hao's letter to Lang had been good news indeed. It proved that the plotters in the palace had not yet got the necklace in their hands. Thus he could discard one possibility he had been considering, namely that they or Mr Hao had intercepted the cashier after the theft and bought the necklace directly from the thief. This theory had been based on the fact that the mysterious Mr Hao had failed to turn up the next day at Lang's. Now it was clear that Mr Hao had been detained, exactly as he had stated in his letter to Lang, and he was expecting to conclude the deal tonight, in Lang's godown. This was excellent. For Hao's arrest would make the plotters in the palace pause and ponder for a while, thus giving him, the judge, a breathing space to concentrate on the search for the necklace. The long morning on the river had made him drowsy, and he closed his eyes.

His sleep was disturbed by many dreams. The distorted face of the bearded assassin again made its appearance; hanging in the air, it was ogling him with its single rolling eye. No, it was the dead cashier who was standing over him, with face green and swollen, bulging eyes fixed on him while mangled hands groped for his throat. The judge wanted to rise, but his entire body felt as heavy as lead, and he could not move. Desperately he gasped for air. Just when he thought he was suffocating, the cashier changed into a tall woman in a soiled blue gown. Long, dishevelled hair clotted with dry mud hung across her face, revealing only the blue, gaping mouth from which protruded a swollen tongue. With a startled cry the judge woke up.

Drenched with sweat, he got down from his improvised bed and poked about among the old furniture for a while, to get the awful nightmare out of his mind. He cursed under his breath when he stumbled over a few dusty bags. They seemed to have contained flour. He brushed off his knees, then stretched himself out again on the hemp sacks. Now he soon fell into a dreamless sleep.

# XIII

An irritating, persistent itch in his neck woke Judge Dee. With
a start he noticed that the barred window was dark. He swung
his legs to the floor and ran to the window. To his relief he heard
the cooks chopping meat and singing lustily. Since no orders were
being shouted, it must still be well before the hour of the evening
rice. Rubbing his itching neck, he found lots of small ants crawling about under his collar. And there were more on his beard and
whiskers, and on the front of his robe. Annoyed, he brushed the
small insects off as well as he could.

Now there was light behind the windows of Lang's suite, and
one panel of the folding doors stood ajar, but he could hear no
voices from within. Two vegetable vendors came into the garden
and made straight for the kitchen. Judge Dee waited till they
had left again with their empty baskets, then he slipped outside
and went to the gate in the garden wall. To his surprise the donkey was still there. It stood close to the wall, nuzzling among
the garbage. He quickly went back to the storehouse and grabbed
the crutches. Feeling safe in his disguise, he rode to the quay.

A mixed crowd was about under the smoking oil-lamps of the
foodstalls in front of the fish-market and there was a hubbub of
shrill voices. Judge Dee had to halt when a cartload of melons
toppled over in front of his donkey. Bystanders came rushing on
to help the vendor collect his merchandise. A shabbily dressed
man grabbed the rein of his donkey. 'I'll get you through, Master
Gourd!' he called out cheerfully. As the coolie was shoving people
away, the judge suddenly heard someone whisper behind him:

'They are after him, but he has disappeared.'

Quickly the judge turned round in the saddle. In the uncertain
light he only saw the laughing faces of a few youngsters who were
pushing his donkey on from behind. The next moment he was
clear of the tumult.

Judge Dee rode on with a puzzled frown. The fight in the go-down had proved beyond all doubt that the old man was on his side. Yet the whispered remark, addressed to him by someone who must have mistaken him for Master Gourd, seemed to mean that the Taoist was kept informed about his movements. What could be the old monk's connection with this baffling case? Again he tried to remember where he could have met him before. In vain.

A thin evening mist came drifting in from the river. Now that he was approaching the far end of the quay where there were no shops or street stalls, everything looked dark and desolate. The only points of light came from the bow lamps of the moored craft that were bobbing up and down in the black water.

When the judge had passed the first godown in the row, he dismounted and placed his crutches against the wall. Then he walked on to the tall trees that marked the clearing at the opposite end, his sword on his back. Just as he was passing underneath some dark branches, a hoarse voice spoke directly above his head:

'You're late. But Hao hasn't arrived yet.'

Looking up, he vaguely saw the huge shape of one of Lang's bodyguards, perched on a thick branch. Yes, Mr Lang did indeed know his routine work. The judge crossed the clearing and knocked on the door. The bullet-headed man opened it at once. 'Glad you came!' he muttered. 'The place is giving me the creeps!'

'Afraid of Tai Min's ghost?' the judge asked coldly. He pushed the bench up to the wall and sat down.

'Not me!' The accountant seated himself by Judge Dee's side. 'Squealed like a pig, you know! A pity the stupid bastards let him die before they had really started.' A cruel smile twisted his thick lips. 'They had fixed him to this very bench, you see. First they . . .'

'I am not interested in your little games.' The judge laid his sword across his knees and leaned back against the wall. 'You can tell me what you got out of him, though.'

'Practically nothing. When the men burned his feet, he shouted a hundred times that he didn't have the pearls. Thereafter he did some more squealing about it being no use going on because he

86

just didn't have them. He died cursing us, the impudent scoundrel. The stupid idiots slit his belly open, to see whether he had swallowed the pearls. Nothing doing, of course.' Looking at Judge Dee's sword, he added nervously, 'That sword might make Mr Hao suspicious. Are you sure you shouldn't put it away out of sight somewhere?'

'Very sure.'

The judge folded his arms and let his chin sink on his breast. He tried to think of nothing, but the many problems he was facing kept bothering him. From now on he would have to concentrate on the dead cashier. For even if Mr Hao proved to know exactly who the plotters in the palace were, he, the judge, could take no official action against them until he had found the necklace. The Princess had especially stressed that point. Again he wondered what Tai Min had had in mind when he decided to cheat Lang. Somehow or other he had the feeling that a talk with Mrs Wei, the absconding wife, would provide a clue to what Tai Min had done with the necklace. 'Sit still!' he snapped at the accountant who was fidgeting in his seat. The only information he possessed regarding Mrs Wei had been supplied by Fern. An uncommonly intelligent girl, but still a girl, and one who had lived with the Weis only a few months. He doubted whether he could trust her favourable judgement of the innkeeper's wife. Fern had stated that Mrs Wei had not committed adultery with the cashier, and Wei was an unpleasant old codger. Yet it was scandalous behaviour for a housewife to leave her husband without one word of explanation. Wei had mentioned a vagrant bully as his wife's lover. That was also a point he would have to look into. He ought to have had a longer talk with Wei, but events had been moving so quickly that . . . 'What are you muttering about?' he peevishly asked the man beside him.

'Just that I am getting worried about Hao. We've been waiting here for nearly an hour now, you know! Why should he make this appointment if he doesn't mean to keep it?'

The judge shrugged.

'Why, you say? Well, he was probably detained by some unexpected . . .' Suddenly he broke off. Then he hit his fist on his knee. 'Holy Heaven, I should've thought of that! Of all the . . .'

'What . . . why . . .' the other stuttered.

'I am just as big a fathead as you!' Judge Dee said bitterly. 'The appointment was a dirty trick, of course!'

Ignoring the accountant's frightened questions, he jumped up, rushed outside and blew hard on his fingers twice. The whistle sounded shrilly all over the silent clearing. The door of the next godown was opened a few inches, and a bearded face peered cautiously outside. Then loud commands and the clatter of arms came from the pine forest. A big dark shape fell down from the tree opposite. Two soldiers caught the bodyguard. He put up a fight but was felled by a blow on the head from the flat of a sword. All at once the clearing was crowded with guardsmen, armed to the teeth. As two began to break down the door of the second godown with their battle-axes, Captain Siew came running to the judge, followed by Lieutenant Liu.

'We saw no one pass here after you,' the captain said. 'The thin fellow behind you is Mr Hao, I suppose?'

'No, he isn't. But he is responsible for the torturing and the killing of the cashier. Have him arrested at once! Hao didn't turn up. Where are your horses? We must get to the Kingfisher as fast as we can!'

The captain barked an order at Liu, then ran towards the forest, Judge Dee close behind him. 'How many men do we need?' Siew called out over his shoulder. 'Four 'll do!' the judge replied, panting.

Beyond the second bend of the forest path six cavalrymen were guarding a few dozen richly caparisoned horses. Judge Dee and the captain took two and swung themselves into the saddle. As he drove his horse on, the captain shouted at four men to follow them.

In the clearing the soldiers were lining up Lang's men and chaining them together. The stolid Lieutenant Liu was personally tying up the bullet-headed man with a long thin cord. Passing by him, Judge Dee called out:

'Don't forget the donkey! It's waiting at the end of the row!'

Then the six horsemen rode on to the quay at a gallop.

# XIV

Mr Wei was standing behind the counter in the semi-dark hall, drinking a cup of tea with two guests. He stared bewildered at Judge Dee and the guardsmen, the cup arrested halfway to his lips.

'Did any visitors come for Mr Lang?' the judge rasped.

The innkeeper shook his head, dumbfounded.

The judge ran into the corridor leading to Lang's suite. The door of the ante-room was not locked, but the one giving access to Lang's study appeared bolted on the inside. Captain Siew knocked hard on it with the hilt of his sword. When there was no answer he threw his iron-clad shoulder against it and it burst open. He halted so abruptly that the judge bumped into him. No one was there, but the room had been thoroughly ransacked. The desk had been overturned, all its drawers pulled out. The floor was strewn with scattered papers. Here and there the wainscoting had been pried loose; in front of the window lay a heap of clothes, torn to shreds. Suddenly Judge Dee grabbed the captain's arm and pointed at the farthest corner. Siew uttered an awful curse.

The stark-naked body of Lang was hanging upside down from the rafter. The big toes of his bare feet were fastened to it with a thin cord; his arms were bound behind his back. A bloodstained rag was wound tightly round his head which just cleared the floor.

The judge ran towards him, bent down and loosened the rag. At once blood trickled onto the floor. Quickly he felt Lang's breast. It was still warm, but the heart had ceased beating. He turned to the captain, his face chalk-white.

'Too late. Tell your men to take him down and then off to the mortuary.'

With unsteady steps Judge Dee went over to the desk, righted the armchair and sat down. Lang had been a callous criminal who had fully deserved to be beheaded on the scaffold, but not to be tortured to death in this beastly manner. And he, the judge, was responsible for this outrage. The subdued voice of the captain roused him from his sombre thoughts.

'Two of my men are searching the garden and questioning the servants, sir.'

Judge Dee pointed at the open panel of the garden doors. 'I don't think anyone'll have seen the intruders, Siew,' he said wearily. 'They slipped inside through there. Entered by the back gate, when the cooks were busy preparing the evening rice. That's why they set six as the time for the meeting. The meeting was a ruse, meant to get all Lang's men away from him, so that he could be questioned alone. I made a big mistake, Siew. A very big mistake.'

Slowly caressing his long black beard, he reflected that the scheme accorded well with the tortuous mind of depraved courtiers, past masters in double-dealing and deceit. They must have a spy among Lang's men, who had duly informed them that the cashier had not delivered the necklace. Therefore they had not sent Mr Hao to collect it. On second thoughts, however, they had reached the conclusion that Tai Min must have handed the necklace to Lang when he had returned to the inn to pack, and that Lang had let him go with the promise of a much bigger reward than agreed upon. And that Lang then had let his men kill the cashier, thus saving for himself their share in the loot, and all further trouble from the cashier. Convinced that Lang had hidden the necklace somewhere in his study, the plotters in the palace had arranged the meeting in the godown, so as to be able to surprise him here in the inn. 'What did you say, Siew?'

'I asked whether you think the bastards found what they came for, sir.'

'They did not. It wasn't there.'

Of that Judge Dee was quite sure. Not because he put it beyond Lang to have engaged in such a piece of double-dealing, but because the cashier would in that case certainly have told his torturers that they must take him to their master—hoping that even if he wouldn't be able to bargain with Lang for his life, he would at least gain a little time.

The judge looked on in silence while the two guardsmen took down the corpse. They laid it on a stretcher, covered it with a sheet of canvas, and carried it away. He felt sick and tired of this insane, utterly frustrating case.

'Oh yes, sir, something nearly slipped my mind! Just when I was assembling my men to go to Lang's godown, my agents from Ten Miles Village, on the other side of the mountains, came back. Mrs Wei wasn't there, sir. And they made sure she hadn't been there either.'

Judge Dee said nothing. So that theory of his was wrong too. He had tried his best, but all approaches were coming to a dead end. He asked listlessly:

'What did the gentlemen from the palace say about my escape from your prison?'

'They couldn't say very much, sir, because I took them down to the cell you were supposed to be in, and Liu had done a truly magnificent job there. I didn't like their mean look, however. Lang's murder gives me a good reason for posting six men here in the hall, sir. With strict orders to let no outsider in.'

Judge Dee got up. 'Excellent,' he said, 'I need a good night's sleep.' Together the two men went back to the hall.

The judge had not realized that so many guests were staying at the Kingfisher. The hall was crowded with excited people. One guardsman stood at the main entrance, the other was questioning a few frightened servants in the corner. As soon as the guests saw Captain Siew they besieged him with questions. The captain beckoned Wei, who was standing with Fern and the clerk by the counter. He told the innkeeper:

'Intruders murdered Mr Lang Liu, and ransacked his suite.'

'Holy Heaven! Did they damage my furniture?'

'Go and have a look for yourself!' the captain told him. As the innkeeper rushed to the corridor, followed by his clerk, Siew addressed the guests: 'You'd better go back to your rooms, gentlemen! There's nothing to worry about, I shall have six men on guard here, all through the night.'

While they were passing the counter Judge Dee told him:

'I'll have a close look at the register. Ought to have done that at once. I don't seem to have done many of the things I ought to have! Well, I'll come to see you early tomorrow morning.'

'You seem to be very friendly with that fresh captain!' Fern remarked.

'He wanted my opinion on the time of death. Could you give me the inn's register, please?'

She pulled out the upper drawer and handed him the bulky guest-book. Putting her elbows on the counter, she watched the judge as he leafed through it. The names did not tell him much. Except for Lang and his men, all seemed to be bona-fide merchants, and all had arrived one or more days earlier than Judge Dee. He would leave it to the captain to go into their antecedents.

'I didn't see you all afternoon,' she resumed, giving his haggard face a curious glance. 'You look a bit peaked, you know.'

'I am rather tired; I'll go to bed early. Good-night!'

Up in his room he opened the window wide, then sat down at the table and pulled the padded tea-basket towards him. Slowly sipping his tea, he made a desperate effort to collect his thoughts. He must review the situation in a dispassionate frame of mind: get over his deep shock at the sickening murder of Lang Liu; see all what had happened as a purely intellectual jigsaw puzzle, and try to assign to each component part its logical place. But too many of those parts were missing. If the Princess had not given him explicit orders to remain incognito until he had found the necklace, he would at least have been able to do something, get things moving. Proceed to the palace and institute an official investigation, beginning with the arrest of the two men in grey from the Superintendent's Office who had been after him. They were not pursuing him because he had entered the palace under false pretences, of course, but because they were in the pay of the plotters. And the latter were determined to prevent him from getting the necklace.

This direct course of action being ruled out, he wondered what alternative there was for him. Time was getting very short. He had only the night and the early morning left, for the Princess would have to leave the Water Palace for the capital at noon. He got up and began to pace the floor restlessly, his hands clasped behind his back.

The lovely face of the Princess rose before his mind's eye. The Third Princess, His Majesty's favourite daughter, surrounded by dozens of court ladies and scores of maids, protected by the Chief Eunuch and his giant-like sentries . . . yet alone, with only one lady-in-waiting she could really trust. The Emperor granted her every wish; he had even taken the step, unprecedented in history, of entrusting her with a blank edict appointing an Imperial Inquisitor. So powerful a young woman, yet so utterly lonely and forlorn! He thought of her large, troubled eyes.

She had given him to understand that the necklace had been stolen in order to alienate the Emperor's feelings from her. But that couldn't have been the real reason. The Emperor was known as a wise, understanding man of balanced judgement, and the loss of the necklace could hardly result in more than a severe scolding. Yet her last words had been that she placed her happiness in his hands!

He reflected bitterly that his over-confidence had led to him making some bad mistakes. His theory about the murdered cashier planning to join the innkeeper's wife had been completely wrong. What had that youngster been up to then, that night when he went to the Water Palace to steal the necklace?

Suddenly the judge halted. A slow smile lit up his drawn face. Caressing his sidewhiskers, he realized that it was, after all, possible to take direct action without coming out into the open.

He quickly opened his saddle-bag and inspected its contents. When he found at the bottom a plain robe of black silk and the long broad black sash belonging to it, he nodded with a satisfied air. It was exactly what he needed. Having taken off his brown travelling-robe, he laid himself down on the bed. He needed a few hours of sleep, but too many thoughts were nagging at his tired brain. After tossing about for a long time he at last dozed off.

## XV

When Judge Dee woke up, the town had grown silent. He reckoned it was getting on for midnight. The sky was a little overcast, and there were occasional gusts of wind, but he didn't think there would be rain. A quick survey of the neglected garden showed that it was empty. The captain's men must be in the hall, or at the front entrance of the inn.

He stripped naked and put on a pair of wide black trousers of thin cotton, and over those the long black robe. At one moment he considered transferring the precious yellow document to its collar, then thought better of it. If he failed, the document would be of no use, for it would be found on his dead body. This time it was all or nothing. After all the fumbling in the dark, all the fighting with elusive shadows, at last a concise, clear-cut issue!

Humming softly, he fastened a leather belt round his waist. The long black sash he tied crosswise round his broad torso, and stuck the sword under it on his back, so that the hilt was over his right shoulder. Then he had a look at the wound on his forearm. It seemed to be healing well, and he covered it with a black plaster. Finally he placed a small black skull-cap on his head.

In the corridor outside his room everything was quiet. While he was walking to the head of the staircase, however, a creaking floorboard made him halt, alarmed. He listened for a while, but no sound came from the hall below.

The judge went down, keeping close to the wall. There was no one in the hall, but he heard the guardsmen talking together out on the portico. Remembering that the previous night Mr Wei had left to call the groom by a small back door in his office, he went behind the lattice screen. He unbolted the door, and found himself in the now familiar back garden. Having left by the gate beside the storehouse, he walked through the alley to the street that ran parallel with the main thoroughfare. In daytime it was a thriving shopping centre, but now all the shutters were up and it was dead quiet. The judge wished he had a storm lantern, for if clouds obscured the pale moon, it would be pitch dark on the quay.

Suddenly raucous voices came from a side-street. Judge Dee quickly looked round for a portico to hide in, but the night watch was already round the corner and challenged him. The sergeant lifted his storm-lantern.

'Aha, Doctor Liang! You are out late, Doctor! Anything we can do for you?'

'I was called out for a difficult delivery, near the fish-market.'

'We can't help you there, Doctor!' the sergeant said. His men guffawed.

'What you can do,' the judge remarked, 'is lend me your lantern.'

'You're welcome!' The soldiers marched off.

Judge Dee put the lantern out, for he might badly need it later on. When he was getting near to the quay he looked over his shoulder a few times, for he had the uneasy feeling that he was being stared at. But all the windows were shuttered, and he saw nothing move among the shadows between the houses.

The east end of the quay was shrouded in a grey mist. Letting himself be guided by the oil-lamps of the boats, he reached the waterside. As he was looking over the long row of craft moored there he wondered which boat would be Fern's. They all looked alike in the darkness.

'It's the fifth from the left,' a small voice spoke behind him.

The judge swung round, and frowned at the slender black figure. 'So it's you! Why are you following me?'

'Your own fault, for you kept me awake! My attic is right over your room, you see, and I, too, had planned to make it an early night. First I heard you stamping around, and then you began to toss about on your bed! I couldn't get any sleep, and when you made the floorboard in the corridor creak I thought I'd better follow you and see what you were up to. Quite rightly too, as it turns out, for I certainly don't want to see my boat founder. I am rather fond of it.'

95

'Listen, Fern, this nonsense must stop! You go back home at once. I know what I am doing.'

'Not in a boat you don't! Where are you bound for?'

'I'm not going far, if you must know. The fourth cove upstream.'

She sniffed.

'Think you could ever find that, in the dark? Believe me, you can hardly see the mouth even in broad daylight! Very narrow, and clogged with water-weeds. I happen to know that cove, because there are good crabs there. Come along, step inside!'

The judge hesitated. She was right; it might take him hours to find the cove. If she was prepared to wait where she was, she wouldn't be in any danger, and it would save him no end of trouble.

'I want to have a look around in the forest there. You may have to wait several hours, you know.'

'I can sleep in my boat as comfortably as in my bed. There are tall pine trees all around that cove and I'll moor the boat under the branches. I have a canvas sheet in the boat in case we get rain, but I don't think it'll be more than a few showers.'

He sat down in the stern. 'You are really a great help, Fern!' he said gratefully as she was poling the boat out.

'I like you. And what's more, I trust you. For only heaven knows what you mean by gadding about this time of the night! We won't light the lantern at the bow, anyway.'

When they were out in the open water, a cloud obscured the moon and it was pitch dark. He realized that without her he would have been utterly lost. She moved the sculling oar in a quick rhythm, but so deftly that the boat sped on with hardly a noise. A sudden chilly gust of wind blew over the water, and he pulled his robe close to his bare breast.

'Here we are!'

She turned the boat into a narrow inlet, the overhanging branches brushing his shoulders. A dark mass of high trees loomed ahead. She took the pole, and soon he felt the hull scrape against rocks.

'I'll put her alongside this rocky ledge,' she announced. 'You can light your lantern now; no one can see us from the river.'

Judge Dee took his tinderbox from his sleeve and lit the storm-lantern borrowed from the night watch. Now he saw Fern was wearing a black jacket and black trousers, and had a black scarf wound round her hair. With a mischievous glint in her large eyes, she remarked:

'You see I know the proper dress for a nightly escapade! Well, we enjoy complete privacy in this sheltered cove. Just you and me and mother moon. Don't you feel like whispering in my little ear what this is all about?'

'I want to look for something, along the old footpath that crosses the forest. It'll take me at least a couple of hours. If I am not back by three, return to the town alone. I warn you it'll be a long wait.'

'Next thing you'll tell me is that you want to look for medicinal herbs!' she snapped. 'Well, don't mind me, mind the snakes. Better light the way well, so as not to step on one. They don't like that.'

Judge Dee tucked the slips of his long robe under his belt and waded ashore. Taking the lantern in his left hand, he poked about in the dense undergrowth with his sword, looking for a gap.

'The perfect highwayman!' Fern called out behind him. 'Good luck!'

With a wry smile the judge struggled with lanky branches and thorny shrubs, keeping in a north-easterly direction. Sooner than he had expected he came out on a narrow path. To his right it disappeared in a mass of tangled weeds, but to the left it was fairly clear. The judge selected a thick, dead branch and laid it across the path, so as not to miss the spot when he came back. If he came back, rather.

After he had followed the winding path for a while he noticed that the night wasn't so quiet any more. There was a constant rustling among the thick undergrowth lining the path on either side, alternated with squeaks and growls, and night-birds called out in the dark branches overhead. Now and then sounded the melancholy hooting of an owl. Small animals scuttled away from the light the lantern threw in front of his boots, but he didn't see any snakes. 'Probably only mentioned them to tease me!' he muttered with a smile. She was a plucky girl. All at once he halted and stepped back quickly. A spotted snake about five feet long slithered across the path. Plucky, and truthful too, he reflected sourly.

Walking through the eerie pine forest he soon lost his sense of time. After what he estimated to be about half an hour, the path broadened out somewhat, and there was a glimmer of light among the trees ahead. Then he saw the water, and across it the massive bulk of the north-west watch-tower. It's left corner rose up from the river, a silent mass of water, very black under the overcast sky.

The footpath bent to the right, running directly south along the west moat of the Water Palace. Going down on his knees, he crept through the row of low trees and shrubs that separated him from the brink of the moat. When he was crouching right on the water's edge, he discovered to his dismay that the moat was much broader than it had looked from midstream that morning. He had estimated it then at about fifteen feet, but actually it was nearer to thirty or forty. The still, dark water a few feet below him looked singularly uninviting, and he could discern no trace of the sluice-door under its opaque surface. Up to now, however, Mr Hao's instructions, which the bullet-headed accountant had reeled off, had proved correct.

He took a thin, dry branch from the underwood, leaned forward and explored the water. Yes, there was indeed a broad beam there, about three feet under the surface. Suddenly shouted orders came from the battlement of the watch-tower, followed by the clatter of iron boots on stone, very loud in the still night. The judge quickly ducked under the branches. The watch was being relieved, which meant it must be exactly midnight.

He crept to the brink again, and strained his eyes. Would there in fact be a ledge along the base of the wall? He could distinguish only a narrow, stubbly strip of muddy weeds, just above water level. With a deep sigh he decided he would have to find out for himself.

Having crept back to the path, he unstrapped the long black sash across his chest and cut it in half on the edge of his sword.

He stuffed his skull-cap into his sleeve, and wound the halved sash tightly round his head. Then he took off his black robe, and folded it up neatly. Having wrapped his sword up in the other half of the sash, he placed it on top of his robe together with the lantern, so as to prevent gusts of wind from blowing the robe away. After he had wound his wide trousers tightly about his calves, he tucked the ends into his boots, and tied the straps round his legs. Finally he parted his long beard in two strands, which he threw over his shoulders. Having tied the ends together at the nape of his neck, he worked the tips up under his head-cover.

When he had crept back to the brink of the moat, he cast a worried look up at the battlements. Mr Hao had said that the archers would 'be busy elsewhere' at the time the cashier reached the palace. The plotters had evidently created a diversion for the archers to keep them from watching. Well, he would have to take his chance. He let himself slide slowly down into the water. It wasn't too bad on his feet and legs, but ice-cold on his naked belly and breast. He reflected wryly that Tai Min had doubtless swum under water along the sluice beam. But he didn't feel up to such an acrobatic feat.

Keeping his eyes and his nose above the water, he groped his way along the slithery beam. His hands met slimy, indefinable objects, and soft, clinging shreds that began to wriggle at his touch. The woodwork of the old sluice door was rotting away and he had to reckon with unexpected gaps. Halfway he suddenly lost his hold. The water bubbled round his head when he went under. He managed to pull himself up again on to the beam, took a deep breath, and continued his course.

When he had reached the other side he heaved a sigh of relief. Crouching in the water, he explored with his hands the muddy strip along the foot of the wall. The mysterious Mr Hao was probably a repulsive specimen, but the judge appreciated his accuracy. For there was indeed a ledge—covered with foul-smelling silt, overgrown with weeds, but sufficient to supply a foothold. Having cast an anxious look at the protruding battlement twenty feet above him, he slowly rose up out of the water and stepped up on the ledge. With his back and the flat of his outflung hands pressed against the sloping wall, he edged along and round the tower's corner. Now he was facing the river, a glittering expanse of jet-black water.

Cautiously he advanced along the north wall, testing every step along the muddy ledge with the toe of his soggy boot. Soon the sluggish, black stream right in front of him made him dizzy; he got the feeling that he and the entire palace were sailing up-river. Resolutely closing his eyes, he forged ahead. He realized that while this means of progress would be comparatively easy for a light, smallish youngster like Tai Min, his own size and weight placed him at a distinct disadvantage. At every other step one of his feet would sink deep into the silt, and he also had to reckon with gaps where a section of the ledge had crumbled. At a spot where less silt had accumulated, he turned round so that he was facing the wall. Now he opened his eyes again. This position had the additional advantage that he could locate grooves among the weatherbeaten bricks which afforded a hold for his finger-tips.

It was a relief when his left hand met the bulging stone blocks that marked the arch of the first water-gate. He stuck his hand inside and got hold of a bar in the iron grating, about a foot inside the wall. Having swung himself under the arch, he grasped an upper crossbar and hooked his tired legs around a lower one, leaving his feet inside the grating, with his boots just clear of the water. It was not a very comfortable position, but he was completely safe, for the upper part of the arch shielded him effectively from watching eyes on the battlements above. He thought worriedly about the number of water-gates he had yet to pass. That morning he had counted eight. Well, Tai Min had done it, and he was following the cashier's course exactly. The only difference was that the cashier's aim had been to steal a necklace, whereas his was to steal an audience. It was the only way he could consult the Princess without disobeying her orders to observe the utmost secrecy. At the same time the route followed by Tai Min might provide some clue to where he had hidden the necklace.

After the judge had rested for a while, he moved over to the left side of the arch, and continued along the ledge, his right cheek close to the rough surface of the wall, his boots sloshing through the silt.

Gradually he was getting accustomed to this unusual, crab-like manner of locomotion, and he felt fairly safe from arrows, for he had noticed that the battlements projected a foot or so. Unless a soldier leaned out far and peered down, he would not be able to see the intruder pressed flat against the wall. Yet he was glad when his left hand, groping for a hold among the bricks, again met the bulging stones of an arch. It was much lower than the preceding one. When he bent and looked inside the barred niche, he gasped and nearly lost his precarious balance. From the inside a thin white hand was clutching the lowest crossbar.

# XVI

With a desperate effort Judge Dee steadied himself. A second look showed that the slim wrist was encircled by a white jade bracelet, carved in the shape of a curving dragon. It flashed through his mind that this was not a water-gate, but the arched window of a dungeon. In front of the heavy iron grating was a three-foot-wide ledge, made of grey flagstones an inch above the water. As he swung himself onto it and squatted down, he heard a suppressed cry from the pitch dark inside, and the white hand disappeared.

'It's me, Doctor Liang, madam.'

Now two thin hands clutched the lowest bar. Below them he vaguely saw the white oval of a face. Apparently the barred window was close to the ceiling of the dungeon, and the floor deep down.

'How . . . why did you come here?' the Lady Hydrangea asked in a weak, faltering voice.

'I wanted to see the Princess. For I need more information in order to acquit myself of the task she assigned to me. How did you get into this awful dungeon?'

'Terrible things have happened, Dee. I have had no food or drink since last night. Get me some water, please!'

The judge unwound the black sash from his head, folded it and scooped it full of water. Handing the dripping, improvised bag through the grating, he warned, 'Dip your face into it but don't take more than a few mouthfuls.' After a while she resumed:

'I am in fact suffering from a mild form of asthma. When you had left, therefore, I thought I might as well take the medicine you had prescribed. But a court lady secretly mixed a vile drug with it. Soon after I had taken it, my head began to swim and I fell onto the floor, violent convulsions shaking my limbs. The Princess, greatly alarmed, at once called the palace doctors who

102

pronounced me mortally ill. Then I fainted. When I came to, I was lying on the damp floor in a corner of this dungeon. No one has come to see me.' She paused, then resumed in a tired voice:

'I know exactly what they'll do. In the morning they'll come, when I am dying from hunger and thirst. Then they'll give me poisoned food and drink, take my body to the Princess and say that the doctors did what they could but that I died in their hands. The Imperial escort is scheduled to arrive here at noon, to take the Princess to the capital. Thus there won't be any time for a thorough inquiry into my death. Could I have another drink?' She passed the wet cloth through the grating.

'Who are these depraved plotters?' he asked, giving her the water. 'That is one of the questions I meant to ask the Princess.'

'It's better that you don't see her, Dee. For in her present state of mind she'll certainly distrust you, assume that you purposely prescribed the wrong medicine. Who are our enemies, you ask? How can the Princesss or I know? Scores of persons are around us every day from morning till night. Every one of them punctiliously polite, eager to please, smiling. Who knows who is a paid spy, or who is conniving at some hideous intrigue? I can only say that since they have now dared to lay their foul hands on me, the closest friend of Her Highness, I think that the Chief Eunuch and the Superintendent, the two highest officials, must at least know something of what is going on. But who knows how things are being misrepresented to them? Who knows how many persons have been bribed to tell the most awful lies, how many loyal servants have been thrown into the dungeons on cleverly trumped-up charges? There is but one person in this palace who is absolutely inviolable, Dee. And that is the Third Princess.'

Judge Dee nodded.

'Both the Chief Eunuch and the Superintendent were markedly hostile when I came to the palace to see you, madam. And the latter is making determined efforts to have me arrested. Who told the Princess that I had arrived in Rivertown and what alias I had adopted?'

'Master Gourd did. Five years ago, before the Water Palace was given to the Princess as a summer residence, the master came regularly to the Imperial Palace, His Majesty having charged him with teaching philosophy to the Crown Prince. The Third Princess often attended the lectures, and she conceived a great admiration for the master. After Master Gourd had retired from the world and settled down here in Rivertown, the Princess often summoned him, for she took delight in talking with him and trusted him completely. Since Master Gourd is so popular in the Imperial Palace, and in view of his advanced age, the Chief Eunuch didn't dare to object. The master must have understood that the Princess is in difficulties, for yesterday he shot a tipless arrow onto the balcony of her boudoir, at the east corner. He is an amazing archer, you know.'

'I met him,' the judge said. 'He is a very good man with a sword too.'

'Of course. He used to instruct the young princes in swordsmanship, for despite his crippled legs he is a marvellous fencer. He would sit on a stool, a sword in each hand, and three experienced swordsmen couldn't even come near him! Well, he attached a letter to the arrow, informing the Princess of your arrival and your alias, and also where you were staying. He advised her to contact you. The Princess called me at once, and said she wanted to charge you with recovering her necklace. Then I sent my daughter to fetch you, for besides her there's no one I can trust.'

'I see. I have traced the thief—it was a young fellow who had been hired by gangsters, and they in their turn had been hired by evil plotters here in the palace. The youngster tried to escape without turning the necklace over to the gangsters, and they killed him before he revealed where he had hidden it. I have not yet succeeded in recovering the pearls.' A cold gust of wind blew in from the water, chilling his bare, sweat-covered torso, and he began to shiver. 'Have you got something I can cover myself with?'

After a while the tip of a lady's brocade robe was stuck through the grating. 'The despicable scoundrels didn't even give me a blanket to lie on,' she whispered. The judge pulled the voluminous robe through the bars and wrapped himself up in it. Sitting cross-legged on the ledge, he resumed:

'The Princess gave me to understand that the aim of the theft was to effect a rift between her and the Emperor. His Imperial . . . I mean . . . well, allow me to dispense with all honorifics, in these peculiar circumstances. Anyway, this very night your enemies committed an atrocious murder, thinking it might give them a chance of getting the necklace. Why should they be so eager to get it? They wanted it to disappear, didn't they? Furthermore, I find it hard to believe that the loss of the necklace would cause a break in the relations between father and daughter. But you are a better judge of that than I, of course.'

He paused, hoping for a reply. As the prisoner remained silent, Judge Dee went on:

'The Princess insisted that the theft was committed by someone from outside. That suggested to me that she feared her enemies had been planning to have the necklace discovered in the possession of a person close to the Princess whom they wanted to ruin by falsely accusing him or her of the theft of an Imperial treasure. As she herself was reluctant to supply details about that person, I won't ask you to tell me who it is. But it would help me if you could at least give me a hint, or . . .' He let the sentence trail off.

There was a long silence. The judge snuggled into the heavy robe. Its subtle perfume contrasted oddly with the foul smell that came up from the dark, damp dungeon. At last the Lady Hydrangea spoke.

'The mind of the Princess is in terrible confusion, Dee. She is perilously near a complete breakdown. She could not possibly have told you more than she did. But I can, and I will. You know that the Emperor stated that he would approve any husband chosen by the Princess herself. Of course three or four contending cliques in the capital began at once to do their utmost to make the Princess choose one of their candidates. For the husband of the Emperor's favourite daughter will be a power to reckon with at court, and could greatly advance the interests of the clique he belongs to. You can imagine their anger and disappointment when the Princess began to show a marked preference for Colonel Kang, the Commander of the Guard—a man who has always kept aloof from all intrigue and who does not belong to any special clique. The opposing factions joined hands, therefore, to make a determined effort to oust Colonel Kang from her favour.'

'In that case there's an obvious solution!' Judge Dee interrupted. 'Namely that she lets the Emperor know she loves the colonel. Then no one would dare to . . .'

'It isn't as simple as that, Dee! The Princess isn't quite sure that she really loves the colonel, or that he really loves her. That's why the theft of the necklace was such a fiendish scheme, you see. The colonel had succeeded in arranging to visit her in secret, and she discovered the loss of the necklace after he had been with her. It was suggested to her—in a very indirect, subtle manner, of course—that the colonel had taken it, that he has a mistress somewhere, with whom he planned to escape to some far-away place. Everybody knows he has no money, and has to incur heavy debts in order to keep up his status. That's the first reason why the enemy is making such determined efforts to get the necklace. It must be found in the colonel's possession.'

The judge nodded slowly. What the Princess had said about taking the necklace off because she feared it might drop into the river had seemed a bit far-fetched to him from the beginning. Now he also remembered that she had laid undue stress on the fact that she had been alone.

'I think,' he said, 'that the Princess loves the colonel very much, you know. For she went out of her way to assure me that the necklace had been stolen by somebody from outside.'

'You can't imagine the conflicting emotions that are tormenting her, Dee. Sometimes she thinks she loves him, sometimes not.'

'Well, isn't that a most common condition with young women in love?'

He heard her sigh.

'Since you are the only man who could still save the situation, Dee, I shall also tell you now the second reason why the despicable plotters are so keen on the necklace as a means of stirring up trouble between the Princess and the colonel. It is so terrible a secret that in ordinary circumstances I'd rather die than even hint at the possibility!' She fell silent. After a long interval she went on, 'Hasn't it ever struck you as strange that His Majesty never did anything to help the Third Princess find a husband? It is the fixed rule that a fiancé is found soon after a Princess has celebrated her eighteenth anniversary. And the Third Princess is already twenty-six! The Emperor's generous statement that she might choose her own husband could also be interpreted as an attempt at postponing her marriage as long as possible. In order to . . . to keep her with him.'

Judge Dee raised his eyebrows. 'Why should . . .' he began. Then he suddenly understood. Merciful heaven! Cold sweat came trickling down his chest. This was terrible, unspeakable. . . .

'Does she . . . does the Princess realize. . . ?'

'She suspects. And there's worse. She is not as horrified by that suspicion as we would have hoped. You can imagine what the consequences might be, should this relation . . . reach its logical conclusion.'

The judge clenched his fists. Now he saw the scheme of the stolen necklace in all its true frightfulness. A full-blown woman of twenty-six, brought up in the hot-house atmosphere of the secluded harem, not sure of her own emotions . . . returning to the capital disappointed in her love for the colonel. . . . If in that disturbed state she . . . if it became a fact . . . then a person who knew the guilty secret could. . . . By Heaven, if he played his cards right, he could practically impose his will on the Emperor! Suddenly he firmly shook his head. He said vehemently:

'No, madam, I refuse to believe this! I could well believe that some such sickening scheme might enter the minds of depraved courtiers—particularly the eunuchs, those hybrid creatures with their distorted personalities, the necessary but horribly dangerous source of evil in every palace! I can also believe that the Princess is swayed by vague, disturbing thoughts, and that she is in doubt about her own emotions. But as regards the Emperor, when my late father was Councillor of State, and honoured with His Majesty's trust, he always described the Emperor as a great and good man, who despite his unique position always retained the elevated character and sure powers of judgement befitting the Son of Heaven.' Then he resumed, in a calmer voice, 'Anyway, I am glad you told me, because now I know exactly what the plotters are after, and why they won't stop short of even the most atrocious murders. But whatever schemes there are afoot, the enemy will be powerless as soon as it has been proved that the colonel didn't steal the necklace. For I am convinced that when the Princess's trust in the colonel is restored, she will petition the Emperor to proclaim their betrothal.'

He disengaged himself from the robe and pushed it back through the grating. 'Don't despair, madam! I shall do my utmost to find the necklace this very night. Should they come for you early in the morning, try to make them postpone whatever they want to do to you. Say that you have important information for them, or whatever you think best. Whether I succeed, or not, I shall be in the palace tomorrow morning, and I shall do what I can to save you.'

'I am not worried about myself, Dee,' the old lady said softly. 'May merciful heaven protect you!'

The judge righted himself and began the journey back.

# XVII

As soon as Judge Dee was again under the cover of the trees at the corner of the moat, he stepped out of his seeping boots and stripped his wet trousers off. Vigorously he rubbed his naked body with the dry half of his black sash, which he had wrapped round the sword. After winding the strip round his waist by way of a loin-cloth, he put on the long black robe and placed the black skull-cap on his head. At a loss what to do with the wet trousers, he finally threw them into a rabbit hole. Then he took up the lantern and the sword.

Bodily comfort pervaded him with a luxurious feeling of ease. But he suddenly realized that his head was empty. Reaction to the tense hour he had just spent had set in. As he followed the path through the forest he felt utterly unable to even try to digest all he had learned. Remembering Master Gourd's words about the importance of being empty, he gave up trying to concentrate, and just imagined he was the cashier Tai Min, going back along this same path, with a necklace he wanted to hide somewhere. Walking on, the judge noticed that although his mind was numb, his senses were abnormally alert. He keenly perceived all the odours of the forest, his ears were attuned to every sound that came from the dark foliage, and his eyes spotted every hollow in the tree-trunks, every hole in the mossy boulders that came within the lighted circle of his lantern. He briefly explored those spots that might have attracted the cashier's attention, but the necklace was not there.

After about an hour he barked his shins on the dead branch he had put across the path. He was glad he had thus marked his point of departure, for the trees and the brush looked alike everywhere. He parted the branches and picked his way through the undergrowth to the bank of the cove.

While walking through the forest under the canopy of the

high trees, he had not noticed that the moon had come out. Now its soft light shone on the still water of the cove. Standing on the rocky ledge, he stared astonished at the boat, moored under the overhanging branches of a gnarled pine tree. Fern wasn't inside. Then there was a splashing sound behind him and she called out:

'You're back early! You've hardly been two hours, you know!'

He turned round. Fern was standing naked in the knee-deep pool, drops of water glistening on her splendid young body. Her breathtaking beauty made the blood surge in his veins, touched his stimulated senses to the raw. She squatted down in the water and covered her breasts with her arms.

'You look awful! You should take a dip too!'

'Sorry to have kept you waiting,' he muttered and sat down on the ledge, his back towards her. 'Better get dressed, it's long past midnight.' He took off his boots, pulled a handful of grass from between the stones and wetted it in the water.

'I didn't mind waiting at all,' she said, coming closer. Out of the corner of his eye he saw her standing upright near the ledge, wringing out her long tresses.

'Hurry up!' he told her and began to scrub his muddy boots with unnecessary vigour.

He took his time cleaning them. When he had put them on again and got up, she was dressed, and busy pulling the boat from under the pine tree. The judge stepped inside, and she poled the boat towards the mouth of the cove. Taking up the sculling oar, she cast a forlorn look at the silvery pine trees and said, in a small voice:

'I am sorry, sir. I behaved like a silly girl. But the fact is that I like you, and I had hoped you would take me with you to the capital.'

He leaned back in the bow. The empty feeling in his head had gone; he was only tired now, very tired. After a while he said:

'You like me only because I remind you of the happy, sheltered life at home with your father, Fern. Since I like you too, I want to see you happy with some nice young fellow. But I shall always remember you. And certainly not only because you were such a loyal helpmate.'

JUDGE DEE SCRUBS HIS BOOT WITH UNNECESSARY VIGOUR

She gave him a warm smile. 'Did you find what you were looking for, sir?'

'Yes and no. Tomorrow I hope to be able to tell you more.'

Folding his arms, Judge Dee reviewed his conversation with Lady Hydrangea. Only after he had digested all the disquieting new data would he try to think of ways and means of tracing the necklace. He felt certain the cashier had hidden it somewhere in or near the Kingfisher. Else he wouldn't have gone back there and risked a meeting with Lang's men. Tai Min had known that sooner or later Lang Liu and his men would leave again for the south, and that would be his chance to come back from Ten Miles Village and get the necklace.

The quay was just as deserted as when they had left, but now the moonlight cast weird shadows on the cobble-stones. 'I shall walk ahead,' he told her. 'At the first sign of trouble, slip into a portico or a side-street.'

But they reached the alley at the back of the Kingfisher without meeting anyone. Slipping inside by the kitchen door, the judge suddenly realized that he was ravenously hungry. 'Have you had your evening rice?' he asked. When Fern nodded, he grabbed a wooden pail with cold rice from the kitchen dresser, and a platter of sour plums. 'On account!' he muttered. Fern suppressed a giggle. Crossing the hall, they heard the clatter of arms in the portico. The guardsmen were on duty. On tiptoe they went upstairs and parted in front of his door.

Judge Dee lit the candle, and changed into a clean night-robe. He found to his satisfaction that the tea in the padded basket was still warm. Having taken the armchair by the table, he changed the plaster on his forearm. Then, using the wooden lid of the rice-pail as a plate, he kneaded the cold rice and sour plums into balls. He ate this simple soldier's meal with relish, washing it down with several cups of tea. Having thus fortified himself, he took the calabash from the wall-table and reclined on his bed, his shoulders on the propped-up pillow. Tying and untying the red tassel of the calabash, he marshalled his thoughts.

The scheme of the necklace had now been revealed in its revolting detail. The plotters in the palace wanted to incriminate Colonel

Kang, so as to eliminate him as future Imperial son-in-law, and so as to bring the Third Princess to the desired unstable emotional state when leaving for the capital. The Lady Hydrangea had mentioned the Chief Eunuch and the Superintendent as possibly being involved in the scheme. But there was a third ranking official, namely Colonel Kang. And about him he knew really very little —only that the Princess was in love with him, and that Captain Siew admired him. But both the Princess and the captain were biased. The plotters in the palace had suggested that the colonel had a mistress somewhere. At first sight it looked like malicious slander. On the other hand one should not forget that his accusers were expert schemers who, as a rule, avoid creating something out of nothing. They would rather give a twist to actual happenings, distort a statement by changing a few words or by shifting the emphasis. Therefore he should not rule out the possibility that the colonel actually did have a lady friend somewhere. The fact that the colonel had not stolen the necklace did not prove that he was not indirectly involved.

Utilizing a scheme of the enemy to one's own advantage was a stratagem taught in all military handbooks. And the colonel had been with the Princess on that fateful night. Probably they had been standing together at the window of the pavilion, and the Princess had laid the necklace on the side-table before they went through the moon-door to the adjoining room. So that Tai Min had only to stick his hand through the window to grab it. What if there had been collusion between the colonel and the cashier?

It was very hard to say what group in the palace was making the attempts at eliminating him, the judge. The men sent by the Lady Hydrangea to fetch him from the Kingfisher had worn the black livery of the Chief Eunuch's office, but so had the other men who had put him down in the forest to be murdered. The men who had tried to arrest him had worn the dress of agents of the Superintendent. All this meant nothing, for they could have been hired by someone in the palace who was not their direct superior. Including Colonel Kang.

It would, of course, be impossible to trace the mysterious Mr

Hao. The one and only clue pointing directly at the plotters was the diversion created in the palace grounds on the night of the theft. He would have to bear that point in mind if and when he ever got round to conducting an official investigation in the palace, on the basis of the special powers granted to him by the Imperial edict.

He clasped his hands round the calabash. These considerations did not shed any light on the crucial problem, namely what Tai Min had done after he had stolen the necklace, and before he had been caught on the road east by Lang's men. He ought to begin all over again, starting with the cashier's motive. Dejected after the discovery of Lang's murder he, the judge, had felt that his theory about Tai Min's motive had been all wrong, because Mrs Wei had not gone to Ten Miles Village after all. Now, on second thoughts, he believed his theory had been essentially correct. Fern had said that Tai Min harboured a deep affection for Mrs Wei, and although he, the judge, questioned her appraisal of Mrs Wei's character, he was convinced Fern was right about Tai Min, a youngster of her own age. The cashier must have come to know that Mrs Wei was contemplating leaving her miserly husband, and he would have told her that he, too, wanted to go away; and that if she went ahead to Ten Miles Village, he would join her there later and help her to settle down somewhere else. Tai Min was hoping that in due course he would be able to persuade her to set up a household with him, and for that he needed money. The silver Lang had promised him represented only a small sum, and Tai Min, being a shrewd youngster, had probably realized that Lang would cheat him anyway. Hence he decided to keep the necklace. Fern had described the cashier as a simple young man; he probably hadn't realized all the implications of stealing an Imperial treasure but had taken the view, shared by many of the common people, that the Emperor was so rich he wouldn't even notice.

That Mrs Wei had not gone to Ten Miles Village was also understandable. She had promised Tai Min to meet him there, but she had only wanted to humour him, to get rid of his attentions. In fact she had eloped with a third person, as yet unknown. A third person who might have been known to Tai Min, and conceivably might have met him when the cashier came back from the palace. These points, however, were immaterial. For no matter who met Tai Min, the cashier had not handed over the necklace. For if he had, he would have mentioned that third person when tortured by Lang's men. He had held out because he did have the necklace, and was hoping against hope to be able to survive and retrieve it.

Judge Dee lifted the calabash and looked at it intently. He remembered what Master Gourd had said about the importance of being empty. In order to discover where Tai Min had hidden the necklace, he would have to empty himself, and put himself in the cashier's place. Become the cashier of the Kingfisher, and live his life. The judge closed his eyes.

He imagined himself on the high stool behind the counter in the hall downstairs. Badly paid by his miserly employer, he was sitting there every day from morning till night, his only distraction an occasional fishing trip on the river—a distraction to be indulged in only when business at the inn was slack. But there was a daily diversion, namely the sight of the adored Mrs Wei. The innkeeper's wife must have been about in the hall a lot, for according to the owner of the Nine Clouds she took an active part in the running of the inn. The cashier would have snatched every opportunity to start a conversation with her. Not too often, for his employer would see to it that the youngster did not neglect his duties at the counter for long. Sorting out various bills and accounts, adding amounts with the aid of his abacus, and noting the total down in red ink on . . . Red ink !

Judge Dee opened his eyes. Here was a point worth noting. Tai Min had marked the route to Ten Miles Village in red ink. The map would be in one of the counter's drawers, for it must be kept near at hand, for the convenience of the guests. And up in his attic Tai Min wouldn't have had a cake of red ink, nor the special ink-slab for rubbing it. That meant he must have marked the map while sitting at the counter. By heaven, was that the answer? He sat up, put the calabash down on the bed, and pensively rubbed his neck. He decided to have a look for himself.

The judge went out in the corridor, carefully avoiding the creaking floorboard. The hall was dimly lit by a single lantern above the counter. The clerk had tidied up, leaving only the large ink-slab, a cake of black ink, and a tubular holder with a few writing-brushes. The judge found that the counter had two drawers to the right of the cashier's high stool. He pulled the upper one out. It contained the inn's register, a jar of the thick brown gum cashiers use for sticking bills together, a wooden stamp reading 'payment received' and the red seal-pad belonging to it, and a package of blank sheets and envelopes. He quickly opened the second drawer. Yes, next to the abacus lay a red ink-slab, and a small cake of red ink. Beside it were a water-container for moistening the slab and a red brush. Also a flat cash-box, empty of course—Mr Wei would never forget to empty it before retiring at night. But during the day the box might contain a fair amount of money. He went round the lattice screen. The large clothes-box he had seen Wei rummage about in was still standing on the floor, closed. He lifted the lid. It was completely empty. No robes. And no red jacket.

Judge Dee sat down in the armchair behind the innkeeper's desk. Wei had placed it in a strategic position, for sitting there he could watch the hall through the open-work lattice screen, keep an eye on the counter and all who went in and out of his hostel. Yes, the problem of the marked map had now been solved.

There remained the final problem, namely where the necklace actually was now. He was convinced that the solution to this problem must be sought here in the Kingfisher, and within the small circle of the cashier's dreary, everyday life. Again he imagined he was Tai Min, sitting on his high stool behind the counter, doing his work there under the watchful eye of Wei. He would offer the register to new guests for signing, and departing guests would ask him for their bill. Tai Min would then collect the various accounts relating to the room rent and other expenses incurred, add up the amounts due on his abacus, and write the total in red ink on the bill (which would eventually be stuck with brown gum to the day's previous bills). After the guest had paid, the cashier would put the money in the cash-box in the second drawer, then stamp the bill 'Payment received', and. . . .

Suddenly Judge Dee sat up straight. Gripping the armrests of the chair, he quickly went over all the facts in his mind. Yes, that was the solution, of course! He leaned back and smote his forehead. By heaven, he had made the most serious mistake a criminal investigator can ever make. He had overlooked the obvious!

# XVIII

The crowing of the cock in the cook's chicken-run woke the judge. He got up slowly, for every movement made his stiff muscles ache. Wincing, he went through a few of the exercises boxers use for regulating the blood circulation. Then he put on the long black robe of the preceding night, and placed the small skull-cap on his head. The folded yellow document he put in his sleeve.

As he came down the stairs he saw to his surprise about a dozen guardsmen loitering in the hall. Siew's tall lieutenant was leaning against the counter, leisurely drinking a cup of tea with the innkeeper. Liu came to meet the judge, saluted and said with a faint smile:

'I saw in this morning's report of the night watch that you were called away in the deep of night, Doctor. It was a boy, I hope?' When Judge Dee nodded he went on, 'I am glad to hear that, for the parents. I remember how glad I was when my first turned out to be a boy.' He scratched his nose, a habit copied from his captain. 'Well, the captain told me you planned to visit him first thing this morning, and ordered me to fetch you. Then we saw four gentlemen in the square—in black, this time, not in grey. All kinds of riff-raff are roaming the streets nowadays, so the captain thought we'd better provide an escort, sir. The captain wouldn't like you to have an accident, you see.'

'Thanks very much. Let's be on our way. I have urgent business with the captain.'

Stepping out on the portico, he saw four men dressed in black robes in front of the Nine Clouds, talking to the portly host, who was looking even more dyspeptic than before. When they saw the judge appear they started to cross the street. But then Liu and his men came marching out of the door and they quickly went back.

The judge and Liu found Captain Siew eating a large bowl of

noodles with gusto. He laid down his chopsticks and made to get up, but Judge Dee said quickly:

'Stay where you are! I am in a great hurry. First, many thanks for the timely escort. Second, I want you to have the yellow Imperial standard hoisted here in front of your office.' He took the yellow paper from his sleeve and smoothed it out on the desk.

The captain took in the contents at a glance. He nearly overturned his chair in his hurry to get up. 'This, sir . . . I mean, Excellency, I . . .'

'Give the necessary orders at once, Captain. Let the incomparable Liu here bring me a flat-iron and a piece of the best yellow silk!'

Captain Siew and his assistant rushed outside. The hoisting of the yellow standard meant that a high official with personal orders from the Emperor was present. It implied that that section of the town would be cordoned off by guardsmen, and that the inhabitants must put up the shutters and stay inside.

The lieutenant came back first. Judge Dee took the flat-bottomed brass pan heaped with glowing coals by its long handle, and ironed the Imperial edict. When he had rolled the paper up in the yellow silk, Captain Siew came inside and reported that the standard had been hoisted and all prescribed measures taken.

'Good. You will ride at once to the palace, Siew, show the Imperial Words to your colonel, and go together with him to the Superintendent. Tell them that the Imperial Inquisitor orders both of them to repair to this office at once, and with the minimum retinue, to be received in audience in the court hall downstairs. I would like to summon the Chief Eunuch too, but the palace rules forbid him to leave his post under any circumstances. Tell them that I order the utmost secrecy, and you will see to it personally that neither the colonel nor the Superintendent destroy, or order to be destroyed, any papers or notes in their respective offices. You shall add that the Inquisitor is concerned about the illness of the Lady Hydrangea, and that he trusts that the palace doctors have effected a complete cure. Return my identity paper to me!'

After the captain had unlocked his drawer and handed the document to the judge with a bow, the latter resumed: 'We'd better do everything in the proper way. You'll order the Super-intendent to supply you with a Censor's cap, and the yellow stole. I'll dispense with the robes. Bring cap and stole in to me before you admit my visitors to the court hall. Hurry up, we have a busy morning before us!'

Captain Siew was so perplexed by all these unexpected happenings that he couldn't formulate even one of all the questions that came to his lips. Making a bubbling noise, he accepted the yellow roll respectfully in both hands and rushed out. Judge Dee told the lieutenant who was standing stiffly at attention:

'First of all I want you to get me a bowl of those nice noodles, Liu!'

After the judge had enjoyed a leisurely breakfast seated at the captain's desk, he told Liu to take him to the court hall downstairs.

The court was not as large as an ordinary civilian tribunal, but on the platform at the back stood the usual high bench covered with a scarlet cloth, and beside it a small desk for the military scribe. Against the wall behind the bench was a high table, bearing a bronze incense-burner. The stone-flagged floor was bare.

'Take away the low desk, Liu, and place an armchair on the right and left of the bench. Bring me a large pot of hot tea!'

The judge sat down in the armchair behind the bench. When the lieutenant had brought a large tea-pot of blue and white porcelain and had poured a cup, the judge ordered him to wait outside. He was to see to it that no one entered the hall except the Superintendent, the colonel and Captain Siew. Then Judge Dee leaned back in his chair and, slowly caressing his sidewhiskers, surveyed the empty hall. It reminded him of his own court hall in the tribunal of Poo-yang. If everything went well, he could be back there in a day or two.

After Judge Dee had emptied several cups of tea, Captain Siew came and handed the yellow roll to him. The judge rose, lit the incense in the bronze burner, and laid the yellow roll in front of it, the place of honour reserved for Imperial edicts. The captain opened the bundle wrapped up in red silk. Judge Dee exchanged his skull-cap for the high winged cap of black velvet, braided with gold, the front decorated with the golden insignia of his present exalted rank. After he had draped the broad yellow stole round his shoulders, he resumed his seat and told the captain the audience could begin.

The double-doors were thrown open, and the Superintendent strode inside, magnificent in his wide ceremonial robe of violet brocade, embroidered in gold, and wearing a high, three-layered cap on his head. He was followed by the colonel, resplendent in his gilt coat of mail with the beautifully chiselled breast- and shoulder-plates. Both made a low bow, the long coloured plumes on the colonel's golden helmet sweeping the floor. Then they advanced to the front of the bench, and knelt on the stone floor.

'You may rise,' Judge Dee told them curtly. 'This is a quite informal audience. You are allowed, therefore, to take those arm-chairs at the bench. The captain shall stand by the door and see to it that we are not disturbed.'

His two guests seated themselves stiffly. Colonel Kang laid his broadsword across his knees. Judge Dee slowly emptied his teacup, then he sat up straight and spoke:

'His Imperial Majesty has deigned to charge me with the investigation of some irregularities that have recently occurred in the Water Palace—irregularities culminating in the disappearance of an Imperial Treasure, the pearl necklace belonging to Her Imperial Highness the Third Princess. You two and the Chief Eunuch, being the three highest officials in the Water Palace, are held responsible. I need not, I trust, remind you of the extreme gravity of the situation.'

The two men bowed.

'I have now completed my investigation and we shall presently proceed to the palace where I shall order the Chief Eunuch to request an audience with Her Imperial Highness, so as to enable me to present my report. However, it so happens that the theft of the necklace is narrowly linked with another atrocious crime committed here in Rivertown. In order to clarify the complex situation, I want first to dispose of that murder case in your presence.' Rising he added, 'I invite you to accompany me to the inn of the Kingfisher.'

## XIX

In the empty street two colossal, brocade-curtained palankeens stood waiting, each manned by a dozen bearers. In front of them, and behind, platoons of guardsmen had taken up position, armed to the teeth and holding their long halberds high.

Judge Dee entered the Superintendent's palankeen and motioned him to step inside too. Not one word was said during the short journey to the Kingfisher.

Mr Wei stood in the hall together with a dozen or so guests. They were eagerly discussing who could be the high Imperial official visiting Rivertown. The judge noticed among them a thin, rather handsome girl, quietly dressed in a pearl-grey gown. By her side stood an elegant-looking youngster, wearing a black scholar's cap. He had a moon-guitar under his arm, in a brocade cover. The judge surmised that this was the musical couple that occupied the room below his. He turned to Captain Siew, who had rushed ahead to the inn on foot together with his stolid lieutenant. 'Clear the hall!' Judge Dee ordered. 'Have your men fetch three armchairs, and place them against the back wall.'

The judge seated himself in the chair in the middle, and motioned the Superintendent and Colonel Kang to take the chairs on his right and left. Then he told the captain: 'Lead the innkeeper Wei Cheng before me!'

Two guardsmen led the innkeeper inside. He gaped at the three high officials in astonishment. The soldiers pressed him down on his knees.

'Two weeks ago,' the judge informed his companions, 'this man reported that his wife had absconded with a secret lover.'

The Superintendent tugged angrily at his grey goatee.

'Are you quite sure, Excellency, that this sordid affair of a lowly innkeeper really does concern us, the highest . . .'

'Quite sure,' Judge Dee interrupted. He addressed Wei harshly:

'You are a miser, Wei. In itself that is not a crime. But it may lead to a crime. In your case, it led to a heinous murder. You can't bear to part with your money, Wei, nor could you bear to part with your wife. You didn't love her, but she was your property, and you were not going to let others take your property away from you. You thought that your cashier Tai Min was making eyes at her.' He pointed at the lattice screen. 'Sitting there at your desk, Wei, you kept a close watch on your wife and your cashier, and you eavesdropped on their talks, here by the counter. When you discovered that Tai Min had marked a route on the map kept in the drawer there, you concluded that he was planning to elope with your wife. I think your conclusion was wrong, but I can't prove that, for the cashier is dead. And so is your wife. For two weeks ago you murdered her.'

The innkeeper raised his haggard face.

'It isn't true!' he shouted. 'The vile creature left me, I swear it! She . . .'

'Don't make any more mistakes, Wei!' the judge barked. 'You have made two already, and those suffice to take you to the scaffold. You'll be beheaded, because you killed your wife without a shred of evidence that she had committed adultery. Your first mistake was that you nagged at your wife so persistently about spending too much money on herself that she often accepted sweetmeats from your colleague in the Nine Clouds. He had given her a few the same evening you murdered her. Your second mistake was that you didn't destroy all her clothes. Here again it was your grasping mind that caused the mistake. Instead of burning her clothes, you kept them to be sold to a pawnbroker. But no eloping woman will leave without some of her best robes, and certainly not without taking her favourite red jacket, which she knew suited her so well.' The judge got up. 'I shall now take you to the storeroom behind this inn, gentlemen. Captain, let your men seize the accused and follow me with the lieutenant.'

Judge Dee walked through the innkeeper's office and crossed the backyard. The hens in the chicken-run began to cackle excitedly, frightened by so many persons in shining garb appearing among the scrawny trees and tall weeds.

123

The judge went into the musty storehouse. He pushed a few broken chairs out of his way and stepped up to the pile of hemp sacks he had rested on the evening before. The ants that had been bothering him then were still there. They came crawling in droves out of a cracked tile in the floor, and marched in a regular army formation across the sacks to disappear into a small hole in the brick wall where a fragment of cement had dropped out. Judge Dee righted himself and turned round.

The Superintendent had folded his arms in the capacious sleeves of his gorgeous robe. His arrogant expression clearly indicated that he thoroughly disapproved of the proceedings, but resignedly submitted to superior authority. Colonel Kang darted a questioning glance at Captain Siew, who raised his eyebrows and looked at the lieutenant. But Liu's eyes were riveted on Judge Dee. Wei was standing between two guardsmen, at the door. His eyes were on the floor. The judge pointed at the wall above the sacks and said:

'Someone tampered with this section of the wall. In an amateurish manner. Fetch me a hammer and a crowbar from the kitchen, Liu!' Pensively smoothing his beard, he reflected that the new white cement among the bricks had escaped him the previous night, in the bad light. He stared down at the empty bag he had stumbled over. Evidently it had contained chalk. As to the terrible nightmare he had when sleeping there. . . . Doubtfully he shook his head.

As soon as Liu had loosened a few bricks, a nauseating stench filled the room. The Superintendent stepped back quickly, covering his nose and mouth with his sleeve. Then the lieutenant brought his weight to bear on the crowbar, and a mass of bricks came crashing to the floor. The innkeeper swung round to the door, but the guardsmen grabbed his arms.

In the hole in the wall was the shape of a standing woman, dressed in a blue robe stained with chalk and crusted cement, her head at an unnatural angle on her breast, the long hair hanging down in a tangled mass. The innkeeper screamed as the corpse began to sag and slowly collapsed onto the floor.

Judge Dee bent down and silently pointed at the two half-

124

decayed sweetmeats that had dropped out of her left sleeve, black with crowding ants.

'I admit that you didn't have much time, Wei,' he said coldly, 'but to immure the dead body without having inspected her dress was a bad blunder. The sweetmeats attracted the ants, and those industrious insects provided me with a clue to where you had hidden the body. Speak up, how did you murder your wife?'

'It . . . it was the time of the evening rice,' Wei stammered, his head down. 'All the servants were busy serving the guests in their rooms. I strangled her, in my office. Then I carried her here. . . . She . . .' He burst into sobs.

'In due time, Siew,' Judge Dee said, 'you'll arraign Wei on the charge of premeditated murder. You'll see that the murderer is locked up in jail, Liu.' He turned round on his heels, motioning the others to follow him. While they were crossing the hall he pointed at the counter.

'Take both drawers out, Siew, and bring them to the court hall. With all contents intact, mind you! We now return to Head-quarters, gentlemen.'

Inside the palankeen the Superintendent spoke, for the first time.

'A remarkable example of deduction, Excellency. However, it was only a crude crime of violence, perpetrated in a low-class setting. May I ask what bearing it has upon the grave matters of the palace we are concerned with?'

'You shall learn that presently,' the judge replied evenly.

# XX

When they were back in the court hall, Judge Dee ordered the captain to place the two drawers on the bench. Then he told him to fetch a large bowl filled with a lukewarm cleansing liquid, and a piece of soft white silk.

Seated at the bench, the judge poured himself a cup of tea. The three men waited in silence till the captain reappeared. When Siew had placed a porcelain bowl and a piece of silk on the bench, Judge Dee said:

'I now come to the question of the necklace. It was stolen by Tai Min, cashier of the Kingfisher. He had been hired for that purpose by a notorious gangster, temporarily residing in this town.'

Colonel Kang sat up. He asked tensely:

'How was it stolen, Excellency?'

'The gangster's superiors had provided the cashier with precise instructions as to how the necklace could be stolen from outside: namely, by swimming across the moat to the north-west watch-tower, then walking along the ledge at the base of the north palace wall and scaling the wall, thus reaching the pavilion of Her Highness. The necklace happened to be lying on the side-table to the left of the moon-door, and the thief had but to stretch out his hand to take it. I trust, Kang, that you'll take the necessary measures at once to eliminate this serious gap in the security provisions.'

Colonel Kang bowed, then he leaned back in his chair with a deep sigh. Judge Dee resumed:

'After he had stolen the necklace, the cashier decided not to hand it over to the gangster who had hired him. He wanted to keep it, and sell the pearls one by one.'

'An outrageous crime!' the Superintendent exclaimed angrily. 'Lese-majesty! That man ought to have been . . .'

'He was a simple-minded youngster,' the judge said quietly. 'He didn't realize the implications of what he was doing. He wanted money, in order to win the love of the woman who he thought was waiting for him in a village in the neighbouring district. Let us not judge him too harshly. His life was grey and dull, and he longed for love and happiness in a far-away place, beyond the mountains. Many have dreamed such dreams.' Stroking his beard, Judge Dee cast a glance at Colonel Kang's impassive face. He resumed in a businesslike manner, 'When he had come back from the palace, the cashier paid a brief visit to the Kingfisher inn, then rode off. But he was waylaid by the gangster's men, and when he told them he didn't have the necklace, he was tortured. He died before he could reveal where he had hidden it. Captain Siew, I shall now hear your testimony.'

The captain knelt down at once.

'Report what you found on the dead body of Tai Min, after it had been discovered in the river!'

'He only wore his jacket, Excellency. In the sleeves we found a package of his name-cards, a map of this province, a string of thirty-two cash, and his abacus.'

'That's all, Captain.' Leaning forward, the judge resumed, 'Tai Min hit upon a very simple but very effective hiding-place for the necklace, gentlemen. He cut the string, and concealed the loose pearls in an object which he as cashier, was handling every day, and which everybody would therefore take for granted. This!'

He took the abacus from the drawer in front of him, and held it up.

As his two guests gave the counting-frame an incredulous look, Judge Dee snapped the wooden frame of the abacus and let the dark brown beads glide from their parallel wire rods into the porcelain bowl. Then he began to shake the bowl, making the beads roll about in the lukewarm lye. While doing so he went on:

'Prior to replacing the original wooden beads by the pearls, he had covered each pearl with a layer of brown gum, the sort cashiers use to stick bills together. The gum hardened, and even a

127

night in the river did not dissolve it. This warm lye, however, should prove more effective.'

The judge picked two beads out of the bowl. He rubbed them dry carefully on the piece of silk, then showed them to the others in the palm of his open hand: two perfectly rounded pearls, shimmering with a pure white gleam. He resumed gravely:

'Here in this bowl repose the pearls of the Imperial necklace, gentlemen. Presently I shall verify in your presence whether all the eighty-four are there. Captain, fetch a silk thread and a needle!'

The Superintendent stared at the bowl, his thin lips compressed. Colonel Kang looked steadily at Judge Dee's impassive face, his mailed fists clenching the sword across his knees.

Captain Siew came back in a surprisingly short time. Standing at the bench, he cleaned the pearls, then threaded them with his thick but very nimble fingers. After the judge had counted them and found that all were there, he put the necklace in his sleeve and said:

'The gangsters who searched Tai Min's body went as far as slitting his belly open, but they never gave the abacus so much as a second glance. For one expects a cashier to carry an abacus. It was the most obvious hiding-place, and therefore the best.'

'If the abacus was found on the cashier's dead body,' the Superintendent said in his measured voice, 'how did it get back to the counter of the inn?'

Judge Dee gave him a sour look.

'I put it back there myself,' he replied curtly, 'without realizing what it really was. It is true that at that time I did not yet know that a pearl necklace was missing, but I should have remembered it afterwards. I discovered it late—but just in time.' He rose, turned round, and made a bow in front of the wall-table. Lifting the yellow roll in both hands, he told the captain, 'You will go back to the inn now, and wind up affairs there.' And to the two others: 'We proceed to the Water Palace.'

As soon as the cortège had crossed the broad marble bridge across the moat, the monumental palace gate was thrown open and the palankeens were carried inside.

In the first courtyard the two rows of guardsmen lined up there presented arms. Judge Dee leaned out of the window and beckoned the officer in command.

'When I was leaving here the night before last in my guise of Doctor Liang, my sword was taken from the black palankeen assigned to me. You'll see to it that it is located at once. It can be recognized by two characters inlaid in gold in the blade, reading "Rain Dragon".' As the officer saluted smartly, the judge told the Superintendent: 'Now we'll go directly to your office.'

They descended from the palankeen in front of the lofty hall. The judge beckoned Colonel Kang, then strode inside. By the Superintendent's desk his councillor was talking in a subdued voice to three courtiers. They knelt down at once.

Judge Dee pushed the yellow roll into his robe and spoke:

'Rise and report about the condition of the Lady Hydrangea!'

The councillor scrambled to his feet and made a low bow, his hands respectfully folded in his sleeves.

'The attending physician reported, Excellency, that the Lady Hydrangea was suffering from a sudden attack of brain fever, not uncommon in this hot and moist climate. She was visited by terrible hallucinations. After sedatives had been administered, however, she fell into a deep sleep. This morning she had so much improved that she could be conveyed back from the dispensary to the apartments of Her Imperial Highness.'

The judge nodded. 'Where is the safe?'

The councillor hesitated but Judge Dee caught his quick glance at the flower painting on the wall. He went there and pulled the picture aside. Pointing at the square door of solid iron embedded in the wall, he ordered the Superintendent: 'Open up!'

Seated at the high desk, Judge Dee went through the bundles of papers he had taken from the safe, slowly tugging at his moustache. He found that the documents comprised confidential personnel reports and other important papers relating to the administration of the Water Palace. Nothing about the private affairs of the Third Princess, nor about the scheme of the necklace. He got up and put the papers back, motioning the Superintendent to lock the safe.

129

'Lead me to your office, Kang. The Superintendent shall accompany us.'

The colonel's office was simply furnished but scrupulously clean. Its broad window afforded a view of an extensive, walled-in yard where a few guardsmen were practising archery. Colonel Kang unlocked the iron strongbox on the floor and the judge inspected its contents. But again he could find nothing that looked suspect. Putting his hands behind his back, he told the colonel:

'Four days ago, towards midnight, there was a disturbance in the palace grounds. I want a report on that, Kang.'

The colonel pulled out a drawer of his plain wooden desk and placed a large ledger before the judge. Each page was neatly divided into small numbered squares, charting the duties of the guard. He leafed it through till he found the correct date, then studied the brief note written in the margin. Looking up, he said:

'Half an hour before midnight the roof of a tea pavilion in the sixth courtyard, in the north-west corner of the grounds, suddenly caught fire. I was in another section of the palace at that time, but my second-in-command sent a platoon there at once and they put out the fire without difficulty. It seems, however, that the Chief Eunuch saw the smoke and sent word that he wanted the entire area cordoned off at once, to make sure that no flying sparks reached the apartments of Her Highness. My man gave the necessary orders to the guards on the west and north ramparts. They returned to their posts one hour after midnight.'

'Can you prove that?'

The colonel turned the page over. A red slip of paper was stuck to it, bearing the seal of the Chief Eunuch, with a few scrawled instructions.

Judge Dee nodded.

'Now we shall repair together to the Chief Eunuch's office, gentlemen.'

The news of the arrival of the Imperial Inquisitor had spread already throughout the palace. The sentries at the Chief Eunuch's office opened the gate wide for the three visitors, and the obese eunuch came rushing out to meet them. He threw himself on the floor and touched the flagstones with his forehead.

THE CHIEF EUNUCH SHOWS JUDGE DEE A RARE ORCHID

'You'll wait here in the corridor,' the judge told his two companions. 'I shall go inside to ask permission to cross the Golden Bridge.'

He knocked at the gold-lacquered door. When there was no answer, he went inside, closing the door behind him.

There was no one in the elegant library. A musty smell of old books mingled with the heavy fragrance of the orchids on the window-sill. Judge Dee looked outside. The old man was standing by a high rock down in the garden, clad in a plain, long-sleeved morning-robe, his head covered by a gauze house-cap. The judge went into the garden and followed the narrow paved path, zigzagging among miniature gold-fish ponds and flowering shrubs. Very small coloured birds were twittering among the green leaves, still glittering with dew.

The Chief Eunuch turned round. Looking at the judge with his heavy-lidded eyes, he said:

'A marvellous thing happened overnight, Dee! Look, this rare flower suddenly opened! Observe the delicately shaped petals, the velvety colour! I had this plant brought here from the southern regions by a special courier. For three months I tended it personally. But I had never dared to hope to make it bloom!'

Judge Dee bent over the orchid that was as large as a man's hand. It was rooted in the hollow of a palm tree, nestling against the rock. Its yellow petals, showing violet-black spots, gave the flower an almost feline grace. The orchid sent forth a faint but very distinct fragrance.

'I must confess I never saw anything like it,' he said as he righted himself.

'And you'll never see the like again,' the old man said quietly. He snapped the stem with his long fingernails, and raised the flower to his nose. Slowly moving it to and fro, he went on, 'When you came here the day before yesterday, Dee, I knew at once that you couldn't be just a doctor. Seeing me with my pet executioner standing behind me, you should've been trembling with fear, grovelling even. Instead you calmly exchanged profound remarks with me, as if with your equal. Next time you put on a disguise, take care that you also disguise your personality, Dee!'

132

'You made determined efforts to have me eliminated,' the judge remarked. 'But luck was on my side, and I shall presently return the pearl necklace to Her Imperial Highness. Therefore I ask your permission to cross the Golden Bridge.'

The old man turned the flower round in his thin hand.

'Don't misunderstand me, Dee. Yes, I did want power. The well-nigh unlimited power possessed by him who knows an Emperor's guilty secret. But I also had a quite different, much stronger motive. I wanted to have the Third Princess with me forever, Dee. Wanted to look after her tenderly, as tenderly as I looked after this rare flower. I wanted to go on seeing her every day, hearing her lovely voice, knowing everything she does . . . always. And now she will be ravished by a brutish soldier. . . .'

Suddenly he crushed the orchid in his claw-like hand and threw it onto the ground. 'Let's go inside,' he said harshly. 'I am suffering from many chronic ailments, and it is time that I take my drops.'

Judge Dee followed him inside the library.

The old man sat down in the enormous, carved armchair, and unlocked a drawer. He took from it a miniature calabash of rock crystal, its stopper secured by a red silk ribbon. When he was about to uncork it, the judge stepped forward and locked the frail wrist in his large hand. He said curtly:

'The evil scheme must be destroyed root and branch.'

The Chief Eunuch let go of the crystal vial. He pressed a bud in the elaborate flower motif carved in the rim of the desk. From the shallow drawer that appeared he took a sealed envelope. He handed it to the judge, a contemptuous sneer twisting his thin blue lips:

'Have them tortured to death, every single one of them! Their miserable souls shall serve me as my slaves, in the Hereafter!'

The judge broke the seal and glanced at the slips of thin paper. Each was marked with a name and rank; then there were notes of dates and sums of money, all written in the same, spidery hand. He nodded and put the envelope into his sleeve.

The old man took the stopper out of the small crystal calabash and poured its colourless content in a teacup. Having emptied the cup at one draught, he leaned back into the armchair, his thickly veined hands grasping the armrests. His hooded eyes closed, his breath came in gasps. Then he let go of the armrests and clutched at his breast. A violent shiver shook his frail body. Suddenly the blue lips moved.

'You have my permission to cross the Golden Bridge.'

His head sunk to his breast; his hands fell limply into his lap.

# XXI

The Superintendent and Colonel Kang stood waiting in the corridor, in an uneasy silence. The obese eunuch was still on his knees. Judge Dee closed the gold-lacquered door. Handing the envelope to the Superintendent, he said:

'In here you'll find full particulars about everyone who took part in the foul scheme. You shall go back to your office and have the main criminals arrested at once. Thereafter you shall institute a most exhaustive inquiry. You may follow me, Colonel. I have the Chief Eunuch's permission to pass the bridge.' And to the eunuch: 'Lead the way!'

When the three men had arrived at the foot of the bridge, the fat eunuch beat the small golden gong suspended on a marble pillar. After a while four court ladies came out of the building on the other side, and the judge and Colonel Kang went across. Judge Dee told the ladies that the Inquisitor requested the honour of an audience. They were led into a side-room where they waited for a long time. Apparently the Princess was still at her toilet.

At last two court ladies came and conducted the judge and Colonel Kang along an outside corridor to a covered balcony, lined by heavy, red-lacquered pillars, on the east side of the palace. From there one had a fine view over the woodland that led up to the mountains. The Third Princess was standing by the farthest pillar, a round fan in her hand. Behind her stood a frail, elderly lady, her grey hair combed back straight from her high forehead. The judge and the colonel knelt.

'Rise and report, Dee!' the Princess ordered in her clear voice.

Judge Dee came to his feet, lifting the yellow roll in both hands. The colonel remained on his knees.

'Your humble servant has the honour to return to Your Highness the August Words.'

The Princess gestured with her fan. The elderly lady came forward. When she took the yellow roll over from the judge, he noticed the white jade bracelet on her wrist, carved into the shape of a curving dragon.

'Your humble servant has also the honour to return to Your Highness the pearl necklace. The thief proved to be a person from outside the palace, exactly as Your Highness deigned to intimate when your servant was granted his first audience.'

The Princess held out her hand, and the judge gave her the necklace with a low bow. Letting it glide through her fingers, she told him, her eyes on Colonel Kang:

'You shall repeat, Dee, the last words I said to you.'

'Your Highness deigned to say that in charging me to recover the necklace, she placed her happiness into my hands.' Judge Dee spoke automatically, for now that he was seeing her face clearly in broad daylight, something had struck him in the line of her cheekbones and the shape of the determined chin.

'Now you know, Colonel. Soon we shall meet again, the red candles burning high.'

Colonel Kang rose and stepped up to her, his shining eyes locked with hers. The elderly lady looked at the tall, handsome pair, a soft smile on her pale, tired face. Judge Dee quickly went to the door.

The two court ladies conducted him back to the Golden Bridge. The obese eunuch stood waiting at the other side. When he had respectfully led Judge Dee to the entrance, the judge told him:

'Go and see your master. I fear he is ill.' Then he got into the brocade palankeen and told the honour guard to take him to the Superintendent's office.

The corridor was crowded with guardsmen and sturdy fellows both in black and grey livery, but all wearing red armlets with the word 'special' written on them, and all armed to the teeth. They bowed low when they saw the judge. He found the Superintendent standing bent over his desk, which was strewn with thin slips of paper. The Superintendent looked up.

'The main scoundrels have been arrested already, Excellency! I regret to report that the rot had spread even among my own men. What must we do about the Chief Eunuch, Excellency? He can't be arrested without . . .'

'The Chief Eunuch died from a heart-attack,' the judge interrupted. 'While conducting your investigation you shall pay particular attention to a person who calls himself Mr Hao, and to close associates of his who last night murdered Mr Lang Liu, in the Kingfisher inn. You shall see to it that they are punished with the utmost severity.'

The Superintendent made a bow. Pointing at his own chair, he said, 'Your Excellency please be seated, so that I can explain how . . .'

Judge Dee shook his head. He took off the winged cap, placed it carefully on the desk, and put his small skull-cap on his head. Then he divested himself of the yellow stole, and placed it beside the cap.

'I have returned the August Words to Her Highness. From now on I am just the magistrate of Poo-yang. I leave everything in your capable hands, sir.'

The Superintendent fixed the judge with his piercing eyes.

'Do you mean to say that you won't avail yourself of this opportunity to. . . . Don't you realize that you have a high position in the capital for the asking? I shall be glad to propose that you . . .'

'I am eager to return to my post, sir.'

The other gave him a long look. Then, shaking his head, he went to the side-table. He took the sword lying there and handed it to Judge Dee. It was his cherished Rain Dragon. As the judge hung it on his back, the Superintendent said gravely:

'Your drastic action in Poo-yang against the monks of the Temple of Boundless Mercy made the Buddhist clique at court your enemy. And now you have seriously antagonized the powerful party of the eunuchs. I want you to realize, Dee, that you have embittered enemies at the Imperial Court. But also staunch friends. Including me.'

His thin lips curved. It was the first time Judge Dee had seen the Superintendent smile. He bowed and went out. The lieutenant at the gate asked him whether he wanted a palankeen, but the judge said he preferred a horse. The gates were thrown open and he rode across the marble bridge.

# XXII

Entering the pine forest, Judge Dee felt the warm rays of the sun on his back. He realized it was getting on for noon. Deeply inhaling the bracing air, he reflected that this was a nice change after the hectic, hothouse atmosphere of the Water Palace. Squaring his shoulders, he thought proudly of the Dragon Throne, unsullied by infamous insinuations. There would always be all kinds of intrigues in the palace—it was an unavoidably weak point in the administration of this great country. But as long as the top remained sound, all was well under Heaven. He rode along, the hoofs of his horse treading noiselessly on the thick layer of pine-needles covering the road.

Suddenly he reined in his horse. Master Gourd came riding round the bend, hunched up on his donkey, his crutches across its rump. The calabash was hanging from his belt by a red-tasselled cord. Halting his mount, the old man surveyed the judge from under his tufted eyebrows.

'Glad to see you wearing that skull-cap, magistrate. I knew that a scrap of yellow paper with a blob of red ink on it couldn't change your nature. Where's your calabash?'

'I left it at the Kingfisher. I am very glad to meet you once more before leaving Rivertown, Master Gourd.'

'This is the third time and the last, magistrate. Just like nature, man's life revolves in cycles. For one brief moment yours and mine touched. What's the news from the palace?'

'I returned your daughter's necklace. I expect her betrothal to Colonel Kang will be announced in the near future. Who are you, Master Gourd?'

'Were, rather,' the old man said gruffly. 'Since you know so much, you may as well know this too. Many years ago I was a general. When I went north for the Tartar war, I left my secret sweetheart behind, carrying my child under her heart. I was

THE LAST MEETING WITH MASTER GOURD

severely wounded in our last battle: my horse was killed under me, crushing my legs. I became a prisoner of the Tartar barbarians; for fifteen long years I was their meanest slave. That made me realize the emptiness of worldly power. I would have killed myself, but thinking of her made me cling to life, miserable as it was. When I succeeded in escaping and returned to China, my sweetheart was dead. She had been elected Imperial Consort just after I had left, and in due time had borne a daughter. My daughter, as you correctly surmised. She was recorded as the Emperor's own child, because the eunuchs feared to be punished for not having ascertained she was a virgin upon entering the harem. That, magistrate, showed me the emptiness of worldly love. Thus I became a vagrant monk, with only one link left with this world, namely my concern for my daughter's happiness.' He paused, then added, reluctantly, 'My name was Ou-yang Pei-han.'

Judge Dee nodded slowly. He had heard of the famous, dashing general. His death in battle had been mourned by the entire nation. Twenty-five years ago.

The old man resumed:

'A gourd becomes useful only after it has been emptied. For then its dry rind may serve as a container. The same goes for us, magistrate. It's only after we have been emptied of all our vain hopes, all our petty desires and cherished illusions, that we can be useful to others. Perhaps you'll realize this later, magistrate, when you are older. Well, when I met you in the forest, I recognized you, for I had heard it said that we resemble each other, and I sensed the force of your personality. It so happened that the gourds we were carrying formed the first link between us, establishing our relationship of travelling-doctor and vagrant monk in a spontaneous, quite natural manner. And so, although I firmly believe in non-action, I thought that in this case I might as well forge the second link of a chain of cause and effect, and I advised my daughter to summon you. Then I just let events take their course. And now you had better forget me, magistrate. Until you remember me, sometime. For although to the unknowing I am but a bronze mirror against which they dash their heads,

to the wise I am a door through which they may pass in or out.'
He clicked his tongue, and the donkey ambled on.

The judge looked after the departing figure till it had disappeared among the trees. Then he rode back to Rivertown.

He found the hall of the Kingfisher deserted. Hearing voices from behind the lattice screen, he walked round it and saw Captain Siew sitting at the innkeeper's desk, writing busily and at the same time talking to Fern who stood by his chair. Siew quickly came to his feet.

'Helping Miss Fern a bit with all the paper-work, sir,' he said, a little self-consciously. 'Lots of forms to be filled out, you know, and I thought . . .'

'Excellent idea. I want to thank you for your trust, and your loyal help, Siew. Sorry I didn't get round to drafting for you a control-system for unwanted visitors.'

The captain looked embarrassed.

'Of course, sir. I mean, I shouldn't have . . .' He floundered, then went on quickly, 'Your two lieutenants have arrived, sir! When they came to register, I told them to go to the Nine Clouds. I'll just make sure!' He rushed to the hall.

Fern gave the judge a cold look.

'You and your three wives! For heaven's sake! As an Imperial envoy, you must have a whole harem, chock-full of women!'

'I am not an envoy but a simple district magistrate, and I have indeed three wives,' the judge said quietly. 'Sorry that I couldn't reveal to you earlier that I was obliged to act a doctor's part.'

She was smiling again.

'We had two nice trips on the river, anyway!' she said.

Captain Siew came back.

'Saw them standing in the hall of the Nine Clouds, sir!'

'Good. I'll take my noon rice there with them, then travel on. I wish you much happiness. Both of you.'

He quickly went out into the street again.

In the front hall of the Nine Clouds, the portly host was leaning against the counter, his face green, his pudgy hands clutching his paunch. He gave the judge a reproachful look. Judge Dee took a brush from the holder on the counter, and jotted down a recipe. Pushing it over to the fat man, he said:

'This is gratis. Take this medicine after each meal, eat often but only a little at a time. Avoid wine, and fat and peppery dishes. And abstain from sweets!'

He found Ma Joong and Chiao Tai in the restaurant. They had sat down at a window-table and were cracking melon seeds. The two tall men jumped up, broad grins on their sun-tanned faces.

'We had two hectic days, sir! Slept in the woods!' Ma Joong shouted. 'Killed two boars, huge fellows. Hope you had a good rest, sir! How did your fishing go?'

'Not too bad. I caught a fine river perch.'

Chiao Tai surveyed Judge Dee's haggard face with a worried look. He thought his master needed a drink. Knowing Judge Dee's abstemious habits, however, he said after some hesitation:

'What about joining us in a small cup or two, sir?' As the judge nodded, Chiao Tai shouted at the waiter: 'Two large jars of the best!'

The judge sat down. Over his shoulder he told the waiter: 'Make it three.'

# POSTSCRIPT

JUDGE DEE was a historical person; he lived from A.D. 630 to 700, during the Tang Dynasty. Besides earning fame as a great detective, he was also a brilliant statesman who, in the second half of his career, played an important role in the internal and foreign policies of the Tang Empire. The adventures related here, however, are entirely fictitious.

Master Gourd is the type of high-minded Taoist recluse that figures often in ancient Chinese literature. Taoism and Confucianism are the two basic ways of thought that have dominated Chinese religion and philosophy; Buddhism was introduced later, around the beginning of our era. Confucianism is realistic and very much of this world, Taoism mystic and wholly unworldly. Judge Dee was a Confucianist as most Chinese scholar-officials, with a sympathetic interest in Taoism, but anti-Buddhist. The pronouncement of Master Gourd on p. 3 is a direct quotation from the famous Taoist text *Tao-te-ching* (cf. J. J. L. Duyvendak, *Tao Te Ching*, The Wisdom of the East Series, London 1954, p. 40). Judge Dee's remark on Confucius fishing with a rod instead of with a net (p. 61) is quoted from the Confucianist Classic *Lun-yü* (cf. Arthur Waley, *The Analects of Confucius*, London 1949, p. 128).

The calabash or bottle-gourd has, since ancient times, played an important role in Chinese philosophy and art. Being very durable in its dried state, it is used as a receptacle for medicine, and hence it is the traditional shop-sign of drug-dealers. Taoist sages are said to have carried the elixir of longevity in a calabash, hence it has become the traditional symbol for immortality. It also symbolizes the relativity of all things, as expressed in the ancient saying: 'The entire universe may be found within the compass of a calabash.' Even today one will often see old Chinese or Japanese gentlemen leisurely polishing a calabash with the palms of their hands, this being considered conducive to quiet meditation.

The abacus, in Chinese called *suan-p'an*, 'calculating tray', is a very effective 'ready reckoner', today still widely used in both China and Japan. Based on the decimal system, it consists of an oblong rectangular wooden frame, crossed by ten or more parallel wire-rods (see the first plate of the present novel; Tai Min's abacus had twelve rods). On every rod are threaded seven wooden beads, divided into groups of five and two by a cross-bar bisecting the frame lengthwise. Each of the five beads on the first rod counts 1, each of the two counts 5; pushed to the cross-bar they count 10. The beads on the next rod count as tens, those on the third rod as hundreds, and so on. The abacus is used for addition, subtraction, multiplication and division. Literary evidence proves that it was widely used in China in the fifteenth century, but it is doubtful whether it existed in this form in Judge Dee's time. A detailed description will be found in Joseph Needham's monumental work *Science and Civilization in China*, vol. III (Cambridge, 1959), p. 74.

As regards the medicine Judge Dee prescribes on p. 36 of the present novel, it should be noted that the medicinal properties of the plant *Ephedra vulgaris*, Chinese *ma-huang*, were known in China long before they were recognized in the West.

The plates I drew in the style of sixteenth-century illustrated blockprints, and they represent, therefore, costumes and customs of the Ming period rather than those of the Tang dynasty. Note that in Judge Dee's time the Chinese did not wear pigtails; that custom was imposed on them after A.D. 1644, when the Manchus had conquered China. The men did their hair up in a top-knot as shown on the plate on p. 111 of the present novel, and they wore caps both inside and outside the house. They did not smoke, for tobacco and opium were introduced into China only a few centuries ago.

Robert van Gulik